J.E. SPINA

IN A
SECOND

PUBLISHED BY J.E. SPINA

COPYRIGHT 2020 JANICE SPINA & J.E. SPINA

COVER BY JOHN SPINA

Car Image by Darius Sankowski from Pixabay

ISBN 978-1-7361673-0-4 paperback

LCCN 2020922768

share this book with another person, please purchase an additional copy for each recipient.

Thank you for respecting the hard work of this author.

This book is a work of fiction. Any references to persons, places or things are purely coincidental.

Names, characters, places and events are products of this author's imagination.

DEDICATION

To my husband, John, for all his support and encouragement and the dinners he cooked so I could continue to write

To my best friend, Fran, who listens to my ideas for new books and supports me

ACKNOWLEDGEMENTS

A very special thank you to my wonderful beta readers, Patricia Bradley, Michele Rolfe, and Frances Stewart for working tirelessly to read and review my work and for their helpful input. Their assistance is appreciated.

OTHER BOOKS BY J.E. SPINA

<u>Novels 18+: written under J.E. Spina</u>

Hunting Mariah

How Far Is Heaven

An Angel Among Us (A Short Story Collection)

Mariah's Revenge (Sequel to Hunting Mariah)

BOOKS BY JANICE SPINA

Pre-School to Grade Three:

Louey the Lazy Elephant
(Mom's Choice Awards – Silver Medal)

Ricky the Rambunctious Raccoon
(Mom's Choice Award – Silver Medal)

Jerry the Crabby Crayfish (Pinnacle
Book Achievement Award)

Lamby the Lonely Lamb
(Mom's Choice Awards - Silver Medal)

Jesse the Precocious Polar Bear

Broose the Moose on the Loose
(Pinnacle Book Achievement Award)

Sebastian Meets Marvin the Monkey
(Pinnacle Book Achievement Award)

Colby the Courageous Cat
(Pinnacle Book Achievement Award)

Jeffrey the Jittery Giraffe
(Pinnacle Book Achievement Award)

Clarence Henry the Hermit Crab
Lucy the Talented Toy Terrier
The First Star

Drystan the Dragon and Friends Series Book 1: Drystan and Durward Save the Day

Drystan the Dragon and Friends Series Book 2: Damara Helps Drystan Find his Roar

Drystan the Dragon and Friends Series Book 3: Delbert Finds Himself

Drystan the Dragon and Friends Series Book 4: Delfina Solves A Problem

Middle-Grade/Preteen/Young Adult:

***Davey & Derek Junior Detectives Book 1:
The Case of the Missing Cell Phone*** (Pinnacle Book Achievement Award, Honorable Mention- Readers' Favorite Book Award)

***Davey & Derek Junior Detectives Book 2:*
The Case of the Mysterious Black Cat**
(Pinnacle Book Achievement Award)

**Davey & Derek Junior Detectives Book 3:
The Case of the Magical Ivory Elephant**
(Pinnacle Book Achievement Award & Readers' Favorite Book Awards – Silver Medal)

Davey & Derek Junior Detectives Book 4: The Case of the Brown Scraggly Dog
(Finalist – Red City Review Book Awards)
(5-Star Review – Readers' Favorite Book Awards)

***Davey & Derek Junior Detectives Book 5:
The Case of the Sad Mischievous Ghost***
(Pinnacle Book Achievement Award & Authorsdb Cover Contest – Silver Medal)

Davey & Derek Junior Detectives Book 6:

The Case of the Mystery of the Bells
(Pinnacle Book Achievement Award & Book Excellence Award Finalist, Readers' Favorite Book Award - Finalist)

Abby & Holly School Dance
(Pinnacle Book Achievement Award & Readers' Favorite Book Award –Bronze Medal)

Abby & Holly Series Book 2: Unfortunate Events
(Pinnacle Book Achievement Award)

Abby & Holly Series Book 3: Secrets of the Trunk
(Pinnacle Book Achievement Award)

Abby & Holly Series Book 4: The Hidden Stairway (Pinnacle Book Achievement Award)

Abby & Holly Series Book 5: The Copper Key
(Pinnacle Book Achievement Award)

Abby & Holly Series Book 6: Faulty Timeline

Table of Contents

PROLOGUE

August

She heard a scream but didn't know where it was coming from until she realized it was her own voice. She looked around and all she could see was darkness. Blinking her eyes she felt a wetness dripping over her face and into her mouth that had a metallic flavor to it. She tried to turn her body but found that she was stuck inside her seat belt.

She took a deep breath to calm herself and think about where she could be and what had happened. Where was he? She couldn't see through all the liquid that was continually dripping into her eyes. She shook her head and her long dark hair came forward across her face and soaked up some of the liquid.

She noticed that the car was stuck in a ditch. She could hear water flowing close by. How did this happen? They were only going for a ride into the country for a picnic to celebrate and suddenly it began to rain in torrents. The road was slippery. Did he lose control?

He had asked her for her hand in marriage. She had been so excited that she hadn't been able to breathe or say a word at first. He looked stricken when she didn't answer right away.

When she finally got her breath she smiled at him and quietly said, "Yes!"

He had taken her into his arms and swung her around in a circle yelling out, "Yes, she said yes!"

She couldn't stop the giggle from erupting out of her throat. She felt content. She had never experienced this blissful feeling before. It was foreign to her. She wanted to keep it close to her heart and savor it a little at a time.

But now she looked around and couldn't find her fiancé. Where was he? Her eyes brimmed with tears that mixed with the blood she noticed that pooled onto her lap. She knew she was injured from all the blood but she couldn't feel anything but a numbness all over her body.

She shook her hair around once again and her vision cleared a little more, enough to see that there was a body lying next to her. There was so much blood all over his face, and his head was at a strange angle. She began to scream over and over again.

CHAPTER ONE

A Month Later

"How are you feeling?"

The woman in the bed opened her eyes and looked at the person in white who hovered over her. She moved around in the bed testing her limbs and felt her face.

"Where am I?" She asked confusion flooding her brain.

"Dear, you have been in a car accident and are in the hospital. I have been taking care of you."

"What happened? How long have I been here?" She tried to sit up and swing her legs out of the bed.

"Now, wait a minute. You are not strong enough to get up just yet. You have been in a coma. Let me get the doctor for you." The nurse reached for the buzzer to signal for help.

Within seconds two doctors on call entered the woman's room and stood by her bedside as they spoke to the nurse.

Leaning over the woman, one of the doctors asked, "Do you know who you are and why you are here?"

"I...I think so and I know why I am here. I was in an accident. But where is Justin?"

The doctors conferred and directed more questions at the woman. "What is your name? Do you remember what happened?"

"I'm Athena. Where is Justin?"

"Who is Justin?" One of the doctors inquired as he exchanged worried looks with his colleague.

"I remember we were in a car accident and went off the side of the road. Justin was hurt. Where is he?"

The doctors spoke softly to each other and turned to Athena. "You need to take your medicine and rest now. We will talk some more after you have rested."

"I don't want to rest. I want to know where Justin is. Is he dead? Is that why you won't tell me? He's dead! Please, please tell me!"

One of the doctors reached for Athena's arm and injected a needle. In seconds Athena was asleep.

"Doctor, what do you want me to do? I can stay and watch over her when she wakes up and asks again."

"Yes, nurse. You need to be here for her until her parents arrive. I called them. They were anxious about her condition and have been here every day since she was brought in. They will be here shortly. Her family doctor and psychiatrist will speak with them about her condition."

***

Mr. & Mrs. Stone arrived a few minutes later and were caught by the doctor in charge of their daughter's case, Dr. Jasper, a psychiatrist/internist.

"It's nice to finally meet you both, Mr. & Mrs. Stone. I'm sorry I wasn't here the last time you came. Dr. Nettles called me in to examine your daughter after her injuries were healed. Now I can work on healing her mind."

"Thank you, Dr. Jasper," Mr. Stone responded stoically.

Dr. Jasper nodded to him and asked, "Can I talk to you both a few minutes before you go in to see your daughter? I have some questions for you."

"Yes, of course, Dr. Jasper. What can we help you with?" Mrs. Stone answered with a tight smile.

"Well, it appears that Athena remembers someone by the name of Justin in the car with her. Do you know this man?"

Mrs. Stone looked at her husband and shrugged her shoulders before answering, "No, I don't. Athena never told us about her seeing anyone."

"Why do you ask, doctor?" Mr. Stone queried with a furrowed brow.

Dr. Jasper took a step back when he saw the hardened look on Mr. Stone's face. "I was asking because your daughter keeps inquiring about him. I was told that she was the only person by the car when she was found."

"Yes. That was what we were told also," Mr. Stone responded without any emotion.

Dr. Jasper continued, "Since it was raining so hard that day there was not much evidence in the car or what was left of it. She was thrown a short distance away from it. Thank God for that. She may have been killed otherwise. She was fortunate to only sustain minor injuries and head trauma since she landed on a huge mound of mud nearby."

"Is that all you need to ask us, Dr. Jasper? We would like to go see our daughter now."

"Oh, of course, Mrs. Stone. I won't keep you any longer. Thank you for answering my question. If you think of anything else you would like to share with me about Athena, please contact me. Here is my card."

Mr. Stone reached forward, grabbed the card and deposited it in his jacket pocket before his wife could take it. He guided her around the doctor and led the way to their daughter's room.

Mrs. Stone smiled warily at Dr. Jasper as she passed by him. She didn't look at all happy as she was pulled along by her husband on their walk toward Athena's room.

Dr. Jasper shook his head over the negative feelings he was getting from Athena's parents. Something wasn't right there. He headed back to the nurses' station to find Dr. Nettles, Athena's family physician.

Dr. Nettles was at the nurses' station desk busily writing in a file as Dr. Jasper stood beside him and waited until he was done completing his notes.

"Sorry to bother you, Dr. Nettles, but I need to speak with you about Athena."

Dr. Nettles was a good man who dedicated his life to helping others. He has wiry white hair and kind blue eyes. He was getting up in age after working in medicine for over 30 years and was looking forward to retiring in the next few years. He smiled at Dr. Jasper who is a handsome, young, ambitious, extremely intelligent and dedicated doctor. He knew if anyone would help Athena, Dr. Jasper would be the one.

"What can I do for you, Dr. Jasper?"

"Can we use the conference room in the back? I would like to discuss Athena's case with you."

"Yes, of course.

Once the doctors were settled in a couple of stuffed chairs with a cup of terrible hospital coffee sitting in front of them, they began their discussion.

"What do you need to know, Dr. Jasper?"

"Please, doctor, call me Nick."

"Okay, Nick. Then you must call me Ash, short for Ashton. Don't ask. My mother loved the name. Who knows where she got it, possibly from Gone with the Wind's Ashley," he sighed and then chuckled.

Nick smiled but his face took on a serious expression as he prepared to ask about Athena's parents.

"I guess that you have been the Stone's family physician for a long time. Can you give me some background on Athena and her relationship with her parents?"

"Hmm, I see you met them today. Yes, I know what you are thinking. They are serious and show no emotion. They have always been like that since they lost their first daughter."

"When was that?"

Ash began to explain about the death of the Stone's first child, Alyssa, at two years old from pneumonia. "Athena's parents have smothered her for fear of losing her too. This overprotective nature continues to this day."

"I see," Nick sighed and directed more questions toward Ash, "Do you know anything about this person, Justin, Athena keeps talking about?"

"No, I never met him. Supposedly, she was dating him at the time of the accident. In fact, she said they were engaged. That is what she told me when she was brought in before she went into a coma. She said he was driving the car and lost control as they took that perilous turn in the rain. So far there has been no evidence of anyone else being in the car. The rain washed away any blood or other evidence as per the police. They were here when she was brought in and questioned her before she became comatose."

"It seems strange that her parents do not know of this Justin and have never met him. Don't you think Athena would have wanted to tell her parents about him especially since they were engaged?"

"Well, Athena kept much to herself because of the way her parents were overprotective. She didn't want to tell them about him for fear they would somehow take him away from her."

"Take him away from her? How would they do that?"

"Well, not in a physical sense, that is. They or I should say her father would somehow talk him out of marrying her by telling him how insecure she is and so on. He did this on occasion in the past. He is also quite wealthy, inheriting money from his parents, and uses his wealth in ways to control people. Athena confided in me about that. She is not close to her parents. Sad to say, but she had no one else to talk to. She called me from time to time. I brought her into this world and she sees me as a father figure."

"Hmm, I see. I noticed that you didn't include her mother in your statement about her insecurity and men in her daughter's life. How does Carla feel? Does she treat Athena the same as her husband does?"

"Carla Stone is a good woman who is controlled by her husband. She does the best she can to keep him in control and her daughter safe."

"Safe? Is Carla abused? Athena too?" Dr. Jasper's brows creased in alarm.

"Not Athena. Her mother is another issue that I will have to explain some other time. It's a long story."

"Do her parents know that you are in her confidence?"

"No, I don't think so. I never told them. I doubt that Athena did either. I did tell her she needed to make some friends and find someone to love her. She has to get away from them. They are smothering her and now more than ever since the accident."

"Yes, I see. I agree that she needs some space from them. Well, I don't want to take up any more of your time, Ash. Nice talking to you. I will keep you informed of Athena's progress. I plan to visit with her after her parents leave. I'll check back later after I see some of my other patients."

"Thank you, Nick. I know that Athena is in good hands. You are smart to stay clear of her parents. I do that myself, especially the father. He is not the easiest person to get to know."

"You got that right, Ash!" Nick chuckled and shook hands with Ash before leaving the room. He realized after a second or two that Ash had said 'he' not 'they' in his last statement about Athena's parents. Hmm, I wonder what that is all about.

***

Nick aka Dr. Jasper completed his rounds and peeked into Athena's room to see if she was alone.

She was sitting up in bed as he entered and frowned at him.

"What do you want?"

"Hi Athena, I'm Dr. Jasper. Nice to see you too," Dr. Jasper chided.

"Oh, hello, Dr. Jasper. Sorry, but my parents just left. I always have a bad taste in my mouth after suffering through a conversation with them."

"Why is that, Athena?"

"It's a long story and I'm sure it would be boring to you."

"Not at all. This is your time now. I finished with all of my other patients. Dr. Nettles asked me to check in on you."

"Where is he now?"

"Well, I would guess that he is looking in on his other patients too about now."

"Oh, I see. What kind of doctor are you, Dr. Jasper?"

"Well, I'm a psychiatrist and also an internist. I am here as a psychiatrist per Dr. Nettles."

"So, he thinks I'm as crazy as my parents?"

"No, I wouldn't say that. I also wouldn't call your parents crazy. I don't even know them. I just met them for a few minutes on their way to your room."

"You met them? Well, then you must know that they are a bit strange."

"Athena, tell me why you think they are strange."

She shook her head and tears welled up, threatening to fall. "I don't want to talk about them. I want to know what happened to Justin."

Dr. Jasper pulled a chair closer to the bed and patted Athena's hand. "Can you tell me about this Justin?"

"I don't understand why no one will tell me about him. He was with me in the accident. He was driving. Now I'm here and no one will tell me anything about him. Why is that?"

"Let's start at the beginning and then I will do my best to find out where Justin is. Okay? You must first tell me about your childhood and your relationship with your parents."

"Why do you need to know that, doctor?"

"Well, I want to get to know you better, that's all, in order to treat you."

"Are you going to give me some magic elixir to make all of my troubles go away?" Athena laughed bitterly.

"I wish I had a magic elixir. I would use it for all my patients and for myself. We all have troubles, Athena, some worse than others. Let me help you deal with the ones that hurt you the most."

Athena averted her face as the tears poured out. She sniffled and wiped her tears away with the back of her hand.

Dr. Jasper placed the tissue box at her side and waited until she had used a bunch to stem the flow of tears and snot.

Athena sighed and thought back over her life and let it play out for Dr. Jasper.

CHAPTER TWO

Going Back to the Past

Athena's mother had never gotten over the loss of her first child, Alyssa, who had been a sickly baby from birth and had succumbed to pneumonia at two years old. Born two years after Alyssa, Athena was protected and wrapped up in her parent's love to the point of near suffocation.

Athena was sent to private schools from the age of five right through to college. She was not allowed to date until she was 16 and then only a few times. Athena's parents were ever fearful of her getting injured or sick like her sister. They didn't allow her to breathe.

The name Athena comes from Greek mythology. Athena is the daughter of Zeus. She is the goddess of wisdom, warfare, handicrafts, mathematics and courage. This fact was discussed over and over again while Athena was growing up. Her parents thought by giving her a strong name, Athena would live up to her name in courage and wisdom. Well, it just didn't happen.

Athena was beautiful in an understated way with long flowing dark brown hair with red highlights that sometimes looked like her hair was lit up by an unknown source. She had brown eyes that turned green or amber depending on the color of her clothes or the light around her. She didn't realize her beauty or the incredible aura that she carried. This aura was invisible to others but not completely because it kept them at bay. She found it difficult to talk to fellow students and had only two close friends when she got to college. Other girls in school felt intimidated by her presence. She was unaware of this fact and thought everyone didn't like her. She considered herself an outcast.

Athena always felt pressure from her parents to do well in school but at the same time not to push herself too much or she might get sick. Because of these restraints she floundered and felt lost all through school. What she wanted to do was anything but mathematics like her father, an accountant, and avoided it like the plague. She turned her attentions to writing which she loved. This was the only way she could express herself, come out of her shell, and write her thoughts down without sharing them with her parents. It was the only thing that made her feel as if she were free.

Justin came into her life when she was feeling depressed and didn't know where to turn. He was a breath of fresh air and made her feel alive for the first time in her dreary life. He listened to her and had a kind way of making her feel important no matter what she said or did. He was tall, lean and handsome with black hair that girls wanted to run their fingers through and startlingly blue eyes that looked right through you.

Justin was a cheerful, energetic, and positive person who always had a smile on his face. Everyone liked him and he was one of the most popular guys in college. Athena had worshipped him from afar during her four years in college. Justin didn't even know she existed, or so she thought.

Athena thought back to when she and Justin had first officially met. She started taking a writing class at the age of 25 when her mother pushed her into doing something with her time. She had told her mother that she wanted to be an author or journalist or maybe a teacher of young children. Oh, who was she kidding? She wouldn't do any of these things. She was too shy and insecure, afraid of everything until that fateful day. She had taken all the writing and teaching courses needed to obtain a position but hadn't moved forward with this goal. She had a degree in Journalism and a minor in Reading. She moved through odd writing jobs just to keep food on her table and meet her bills in her small apartment so she could be independent of her parents. They had offered to help her by letting her stay at home. This she would have no part of, adamantly refusing their assistance.

Athena had signed up for an evening writing class just to keep her mother happy. She also did not want to listen to her mother's constant harping about getting herself out there and live a little. Of course, her mother's idea of living a little was to take a course and not get into any trouble, stay away from men, no smoking, drugs, drinking or partying. Maybe that was why she was so shy and withdrawn. Her mother had kept her locked away in a cocoon so nothing would harm her. Now she was upset that Athena didn't do anything other than write in her journal. Her mother still thought of her as a child.

Athena's head was in the clouds that day as she walked out of her evening writing class. She was not looking where she was going when she suddenly bumped into a body that felt more like a brick wall. This wall turned out to be a tall, lean and handsome young man. Once she regained her composure she looked this man over carefully.

Athena realized who this handsome man was. She whispered softly almost to herself, "Justin."

"Yes, that is my name. Hello, Athena. Nice to see you," Justin leaned down to meet Athena's eyes and smiled an incredibly, dazzling smile that made Athena weak in the knees.

Athena hadn't realized she had said Justin's name loud enough for him to hear. He must have super hearing, she thought. She waited for her knees to stop shaking as she returned his stare and tried to find her voice. Athena had worshipped Justin from afar in college. All the girls were crazy for him including her. She didn't stand a chance with him though. He was perfect in every way while she was anything but. She was sure that he didn't know she existed those four years.

"Oh, hi Justin. How are you? I…I didn't know you were taking this course too. I thought you were going to be a lawyer or something like that," Athena cleared her throat waiting for his answer. She wanted to turn and run away as fast as she could as Justin continued to stare at her.

"Well, yes, Athena. I am a lawyer but I do need to know how to write. I do a lot of that in my job. Now what brings you here? Did you become a teacher or writer or ….?" Justin posed with his hand on his chin as if he was trying to think of what Athena's occupation was now.

"No, none of those, unfortunately. I am still debating at job choices at present," Athena hung her head to avoid meeting his eyes.

"I see. So what do you want to do with your life then?" Justin's face creased in deep concentration as he waited for her reply.

Athena screwed up her mouth and bit her lip as she thought over what she was going to say, "I wish I knew. My parents keep asking me the same question. I know I should be making a decision soon."

"Well, what do you like to do? What do you want to achieve in your life?"

"I love to write and have filled several journals since I was a child. It's my way to express myself and feel alive…" Athena realized she shouldn't say too much. She was opening herself up for the first time and it frightened her.

"Don't stop, Athena. Please tell me more. I think you need to talk about it. It will make you feel better," Justin smiled warmly and waited as he watched Athena's lovely face turn troubled.

"If I knew what I wanted to do I would have done it already, wouldn't I? I keep asking myself the same question over and over again. I plan to make a decision soon," Athena reiterated and turned to adjust her pocketbook on her shoulder looking for something to do to relieve the tension she was feeling.

"How about a cup of coffee to continue this discussion?" Justin reached over and adjusted Athena's pocketbook back onto her shoulder from where it had slipped down her arm once again.

"I…umm, I guess. I didn't bring my car because I walked here, not too far from my apartment," Athena explained as she fumbled with her book and notebook.

Justin put his hand on her arm to calm her. He steered her out of the building to his car in the parking lot at the back of the building.

Athena jumped as she felt a tingle at the spot where he had touched her. She hoped she hadn't shown her surprise and reaction to his touch. She liked the feeling. The warmth of his hand on her arm caused her whole body to warm and tingle. She was shocked at this feeling which was strange to her. She didn't like to be touched normally but enjoyed Justin's attentions to her and his comforting touch.

She let Justin guide her to his car and smiled when he opened the door for her to get in and settled. Athena found herself relaxing and actually humming as Justin started up the car and pulled away from the building.

This humming was noted by Justin as he smiled and put on a CD with background music of Yanni to help Athena feel comfortable and safe. He noticed that Athena was nervous and needed time to think about what he had asked her. He didn't want to hurt her in any way. He had been watching her all through college and did not want to frighten her by approaching her. She was a timid but lovely woman who needed special attention and kindness to bring her out of her shell. He planned to do that and thought over what he would have to do to accomplish this.

Most women in school threw themselves at him and he avoided them as being too possessive. He wanted a woman who did not adore him in that way. All he wanted was a woman who was intelligent, caring and listened when he spoke, really listened, not like the silly girls that attached themselves to his arm and only wanted to be seen with the captain of the football team. Athena was not like the other girls. She was unassuming, lovely, and a kind young woman who listened when someone spoke. She was not full of herself in any way. In fact, he didn't think she even knew how beautiful she truly was.

Justin pulled into the parking lot of The Coffee Pot, a local coffee shop that had the best coffee in town and some delicious pastries and cookies. He planned on having a bear claw and buying something equally enticing for Athena. A sweet is one way to open her heart, he thought.

***

Athena was lost in her thoughts and looked out the window at the blinking lights and the traffic as it swept by. She had no idea where Justin planned to take her and was surprised when they came to her favorite coffee place. She loved the bear claws here. Well, to be honest she loved all their pastries and cookies. She tried not to have them too often or she feared that she would gain weight. But, fortunately for her sweet tooth, she never seemed to gain weight no matter how much she ate.

As she looked up, Justin came around to her door and opened it like a gentleman and extended his hand to help her out. This was a pleasant surprise to Athena. On the few dates she had, the men were out of the car and waiting on the sidewalk for her to get out of the car. They never offered any assistance. This was refreshing and made her smile and start humming.

Justin noted the humming once again and returned her smile as he held the door to the coffee shop for her. The line was long and he directed Athena, "Please go sit down at a table of your choice while I get you a coffee and something to go with it. What are your preferences for coffee and pastry?"

"This is my favorite place, Justin. How did you know? Are you psychic?" Athena couldn't believe how relaxed she was feeling to even say this. She looked contrite at Justin's smiling face as he winked at her. She felt relieved that he was accepting of her statement and actually seemed amused.

"I don't know if I am psychic but I know good coffee as you do. Cream and/or sugar? Now, what is your pleasure for sweets, my dear?" Justin displayed his sense of humor and lightheartedness.

Getting more comfortable as the evening progressed, Athena spoke up firmly, "Yes to cream, no sugar, please. My favorite is a bear claw," Athena couldn't help saying, "yum," out loud. This one word caused Justin to laugh with abandon as he watched Athena's eyes grow wide and her face light up with delight at his response.

"Funny, but that is my favorite too!" Justin added with surprise.

Athena couldn't believe it but this evening was becoming the best she could ever remember having on a date. That is, if this really was a date. Was it?

She looked around at the other patrons of the Coffee Pot. Some she recognized as regulars who came often to sip the delicious brews and savor the sweet delicacies that satisfied any sweet tooth.

Justin waited in line and thought over what and how he would ask the beautiful Athena out for an official date. This coffee meeting didn't count as a date or did it?

He paid for his purchases, picked up the bag of bear claws and tray of coffees and turned toward the table where Athena sat completely oblivious to him coming her way.

What Justin didn't know was even if Athena appeared to be lost in thought, she was completely aware of his presence, and could even smell the intoxicating scent of his aftershave or cologne as it tickled her nose and other places on her body.

Justin gently placed the coffees and pastries on the table so as not to startle Athena. She looked up at him in awe with a sweet smile. He noticed her eyes were now amber-colored, reflecting the lights from the sign nearby.

CHAPTER THREE

Athena felt as if she was walking on air as she went into her apartment after Justin had dropped her off. She could still taste the coffee and sweetness of the bear claw. But the best part of the night had been when Justin had helped her out of the car and kissed her hand after depositing her at her door.

She couldn't believe that she had seen Justin at her writing class. He was so gallant and such a gentleman, even more so than she remembered. If her mother hadn't forced her to take the class she would never have run into him.

Her mother called her at that moment as if she knew when her daughter had arrived home and had just mentioned her name. Maybe she was a witch, thought Athena as she reluctantly accepted the call on her cell.

"Hi Mom. Yes, I'm safely home. The class was okay. Yes, I will go back. Yes, you have a good night yourself. Thank you. Love you too."

Athena sighed heavily and put her cell down on the bedside table and connected it to the charger for the night. She didn't want to talk to anyone else right now unless Justin called. But he couldn't call. He didn't have her number. She should have given it to him.

What was she thinking? She really didn't know him. He could turn out to be a serial killer or something. She admonished herself.

She thought back to their conversation. Most of it was one-sided. He had asked her all kinds of questions about what she wanted to do with her life, how she felt about many things. She never had an opportunity to jump in and ask him the many questions that were flooding her brain.

Why didn't she ask him about what he wanted out of life? All she knew about him was that he was a lawyer who took the writing class to help with the writing in his position.

She tried to think but her brain was addled and numb. All she could see were Justin's beautiful blue eyes. He took her breath away. He was so handsome and not at all conceited. She wondered how that could be. He had been adored by many women in college who had hung on his every word. She had stayed in the background and watched this, not daring to infringe on his time with them.

He had always been kind and patient with all of them. It must have been difficult to do since they never left him alone.

Her cell rang again and she looked over at it and ignored it because it was an out of state number. The only people that called her were her mother or calls soliciting money.

She had not heard from her two college friends since graduation. They were probably busy raising families and married to successful men.

She remembered her two best friends, Fran and Lacy. They used to be there for her when she needed to be cheered up over an impending test or when she didn't have a date to go to a dance. They had once dragged her along with them and their dates to a dance, much to her chagrin. She felt like a fifth wheel. She did manage to dance a few times with some of the men who didn't come with dates.

She snuck out of the dance early and took a taxi back to her apartment. There was hell to pay when her friends found out that she had done that. They left the dance and came looking for her. They invited her to go out for drinks with them after they ditched their dates.

It was a fun night for them. They laughed all night after a few drinks each. Luckily they hadn't driven to the place and had taken a taxi back to their shared apartment.

Athena changed into her nightgown and lay down on her bed and closed her eyes. She wondered what Fran and Lacy were doing now? Had they wasted their lives like she had? Did they have jobs or were they jobless like her? Were they happily married or unhappily single like her?

She jumped out of bed and reached for her notebook that she had used tonight at the class. She flipped through the back of it and found her telephone numbers and names of her friends that she had always kept close by in case she ever wanted to touch base with them.

She grabbed her cell off the bedside table and called Lacy's number first. It rang and rang and finally went to voicemail.

She left a quick message, "Hi Lacy. It's Athena. I know it's been ages since we talked. Love to catch up with you." She left her number and called Fran and left a similar message for her.

Since Athena couldn't sleep she busied herself cleaning her apartment. If she couldn't talk to her friends she was going to get something accomplished. She had been neglecting her place for some time now.

She began in the kitchen and scrubbed the sink and island and swept the floors. She dragged her mop and bucket out of the hall closet and washed the floors. The place began to take on a pleasant smell – lemony and fresh for a change.

After she had cleaned the whole apartment and looked around she felt a warm feeling come over her. She hadn't felt this way often, in fact not for as long as she could remember. She was happy.

She yawned and stretched her aching muscles, ones she hadn't used in a while from lack of exercise. Cleaning was one of those long overdue exercises. She sighed and laid down on the bed. She didn't remember falling asleep until the nightmare started.

She felt herself floating but was pulled faster into a void. It was dark and she felt something wet in her eyes. She tried to push it away but couldn't move her arms or body. She was trapped in a seat. She could hear water flowing by.

She looked around and finally could see someone next to her. She was in a car and the body was…. "No, no, no…" she screamed until she woke herself up.

She hugged herself as she sat up in bed. Her skin felt cold. She shivered and rubbed her arms vigorously to get the circulation back. She couldn't believe she had the dream again. What was going on? Was it really Justin in the car? Is this a premonition of something that is going to happen?

What can I do? Should I warn him? I have been having strange dreams since I was a kid and most of the dreams unfortunately came true. Does this mean that I am psychic like my grandmother? Oh, God, I hope not.

Athena got up and went to the kitchen to make a cup of green tea. She was hoping this would relax her and help her forget the dream. After her second cup, it wasn't working.

She sighed and looked around at her spotless house and pulled out her diary. Sometimes when she wrote down what happened in her dreams they would go away for a little while at least. She began to document the dream of being trapped in a car with Justin's lifeless body next to her.

Athena jumped when her phone rang. She ran back to her bedroom and reached for it but knocked it off the bedside table where she always left it to charge.

"Hello," her voice quivered.

"Athena. It's Lacy. How are you?"

"Lacy? Oh, hi. I'm fine. How are you? It's late, isn't it?"

"I'm sorry. Yes, it is. But when I heard your voice I couldn't wait to talk to you. I had a late date last night. Just got home. It's 2:00 am. Did I wake you?"

"Not really. I was up having some tea. I couldn't sleep."

"Hmm, I see. Did you have another nightmare?"

"Yes…yes, I did. How did you know?"

"Well, I remember how you had them when we were in college. You woke everyone up on the floor with your screaming. We all were nervous because some of your dreams did come true."

"Oh, yes. I remember."

"Especially - the one about our roommate, Gina. Do you remember what you dreamed?"

"Umm, yes. I do. I didn't want to tell her about it though. But after sharing it with you, I felt I had to."

"You better believe it, Athena! You dreamed that she had died."

"I did tell her and she was upset with me about it. She didn't believe me at first until I insisted she not go out that night."

"Yes, you saved her life. If she had gone for a ride with her boyfriend in his new car she would have died along with him."

"I didn't see anyone else but her in my dream. I didn't know her boyfriend was going to die too. I felt awful about that."

"Oh God, I remember how awful it was for her. When she called him the next day to apologize for not going with him, she found out he never got home. She was hysterical when she learned that his body was recovered from his crashed car in the pond not far from home on that winding road. He evidently was speeding and took the turn too fast."

"Oh my God! That's it!" Athena interrupted excitedly.

"What? What is it, Athena?"

"I had a dream like that. I am just remembering the old one about Gina's boyfriend. That's all it was," Athena sighed heavily in relief.

"You had the same dream? I don't understand. Why would you have a dream that already happened and that you predicted a long time ago? That doesn't make any sense, girlfriend."

"I know. It doesn't make any sense, does it? Well, let me tell you the whole thing."

Athena explained in detail about her dream and waited for Lacy to respond.

"Oh, I see. This time you didn't see Gina but instead it was you and your boyfriend. You have a boyfriend?"

"Well, not really a boyfriend yet. We just had sort of a date at a coffee shop last night. I met him at my writing class."

"You're taking another writing class? Aren't you tired of school yet, Athena?"

"Well, kind of, but it was something my mother pushed me to do. I really didn't want to go. Glad I did though or I wouldn't have seen Justin from college."

"Yes, definitely good. I remember Justin. Is he still yummy?"

49

"Yes, he is even more so now. He has matured into a gorgeous hunk," Athena giggled.

"I bet he did. I'm surprised he isn't married yet. Remember all those girls hanging onto him. They were disgusting."

"I agree, Lacy. I avoided him because of that. They were always all over him. I don't think he minded it too much."

"Are you kidding me? He hated it! I saw his face when he tried to get away to go to class. He would roll his eyes with an exasperated look and sigh a lot."

"You must have been watching him more closely than I did, Lacy. I never saw that look or roll of eyes. Wait a minute, Lacy. You said you were out on a late date. How come you aren't married yet?"

"Well, I was engaged but I broke it off when my fiancé slept with another woman."

"Oh no, I'm so sorry, Lacy. Good for you that you broke it off. You deserve someone special, not a womanizer. What about the guy you were dating all during college?"

"Oh him! Well, that didn't work out either. He moved away to take a job and I didn't want to go with him. It was in Alaska, for cripes sake!"

"Oh no! I don't blame you, Lacy! I wouldn't have gone either," Athena chuckled.

"Do you want to get together sometime, Athena?"

"I would love to. I've been lonely for you and Fran. Have you talked to her lately?"

"Not for a little while. She is engaged and going to be married sometime this fall. She said she wanted to get together with both of us. I think she is going to ask us to be in the wedding. We were best buds in college, after all."

"Yes, I remember. I've missed you both. I haven't been able to get myself in gear to find a job. I need to start living. Did you get that job in that big law firm?"

"Yes, I did. I'm not sure it's for me though. But it's a start. One day I want to have my own law firm."

"That would be wonderful, Lacy. You always had it all together. What is Fran doing now?"

"She's a school teacher of first and second graders. She loves it! She's perfect for the job. She has so much patience. That, I don't have."

"I know. I don't either, Lacy. It would be great to see you both. I called and left a message for Fran right after I called you. She will probably get back to me tomorrow or I should say later today. Then we can make a date to get together."

"Are you sure you will be able to drag yourself away from the hunk?"

"Ha ha, that's too funny. We are not a twosome. But I would definitely like to see him again."

"He would be a fool if he didn't call you to set up another date. You are too gorgeous to ignore, Athena. With a name like that, you are a goddess."

"Oh, please! You are too much. Please don't go there again! But thank you for the kind words. I hope he calls. But he doesn't even have my number. I didn't give it to him and he didn't ask for it," Athena sighed.

"Don't worry. Justin is a smart guy. He will get it somehow."

"I hope so. Well, it's really getting late now. I think I'll try to get some sleep. Hope I won't dream again."

"Yeah. I'm tired myself. It was wonderful catching up with you, Athena. Talk to you tomorrow after you catch up with Fran. Let's make plans, okay?"

"Okay. Goodnight, Lacy. Sleep well."

"Thanks, you too, my friend."

CHAPTER FOUR

Athena woke up a few minutes before her alarm which was set for 7:30 am. She had finally fallen asleep without any dreams and felt rested. She did manage to get over four more hours of sleep after the dream and three hours before that. Seven was her magic number for sleep.

She made her bed and went out to the kitchen to whip up an omelet with all her favorites, spinach, feta cheese and mushrooms with a piece of pita toasted.

She brewed her coffee and sat down to devour her breakfast. She hadn't felt this good in a long time. Talking to Lacy did it. She really needed to keep in touch with her girlfriends more. They always lifted her spirits.

Athena turned on the TV and watched the morning news as she sipped a second cup of coffee. Her phone rang and she had to go back to the bedroom to pick it up. She answered as she headed back to the kitchen.

"Hello."

"Athena? It's Fran! I've missed you so much! How are you doing? Married yet? Children? What have you been up to? I can't believe we haven't talked in ages! I have so much to tell you!"

Athena laughed out loud. Her best friend, Fran, was a hoot. She talked non-stop and so fast you couldn't get a word in edgewise. That's why she loved her so much! Oh, she loved Lacy too but she and Fran always clicked right from the first day they met on campus.

***

Fran was first in the dorm room when Athena arrived with her stuff. She piled everything up on the empty bed and looked over at the pretty brunette with the gorgeous hair who was sitting on her bed with earphones on and singing out loud and slightly off key.

She moved closer to her roommate and asked loudly, "Do you mind if I unpack my stuff and use the bottom drawers of the bureau?"

The singer opened her startled eyes and just noticed she had company. "Oops, sorry I didn't hear you come in. I love this song and can't help but sing along. Sorry, I know I'm no Celine Dion! But it sounds good to me! Ha ha!"

"Oh no problem at all. I think you sound pretty good. Hi, I'm Athena. What's your name?" She reached out her hand to the girl.

"Of course you are! You're gorgeous! You look like a goddess! With a name like that, it matches you perfectly! Wow! I love your dress! It brings out the color of your eyes – golden hazel! What's your major? Mine is education. I want to be an elementary teacher. I can't believe how hot it is today. I wish they would put some air conditioning in here. My dad gave me this fan. Thank God for that! Oh, and my name is Fran."

Athena listened and nodded to Fran. She couldn't get a word in because she was talking without taking a breath. Athena managed to unpack all her clothes and arrange her things neatly in her corner of the room as Fran continue to talk.

Fran stopped talking finally and looked around the room. Everything that Athena had brought with her was put away. She couldn't believe it. How did she do that so fast?

"Wow, you are an efficient unpacker and put awayer! I know that isn't a word. But I like to make up my own words as I go along."

Athena laughed out loud and fell onto her bed. She sighed happily. This was going to be a fun year with her new friend, Fran.

"What's so funny, Athena?"

"Wow, you actually stopped talking for more than a second. Now I can say something. It's nice to meet you, Fran. I think we will become best friends."

"Really? I don't have a best friend. There is nothing I would like better than to have you as my best friend, Athena. Thank you. Most people don't like me. They think I talk too much."

"Really? They actually told you that?"

"Yes. Can you believe it?"

"No, I can't, Fran. You are perfect! Cute as a bunny too!"

"You are definitely going to be my best friend. I…"

"What? You actually ran out of words, Fran?"

Athena sat next to Fran and looked at her. She was hiding her face.

"What's wrong, Fran? Are you okay?"

"Yeah, I feel snorky."

"What? What does snorky mean?"

"Umm, it's another one of my made up words. I feel happy and when I'm happy I snork."

"Hmm, I see. You feel snorky and snork. Okay. I feel happy too, Fran. I don't have any friends and certainly not a best friend. I'm really happy to begin college with a best friend like you whether you are snorky or not."

Both girls chuckled as Fran wiped away her happy tears.

"Do you want to go out to the hamburger place on the corner? I saw a lot of people gathering there. It must be pretty good, huh?"

"It is, Athena. I went there yesterday right after I moved in. It was dynamite! Let's go."

Arm in arm the two new best friends ventured out for a quick dinner.

***

Athena came back to the present when she no longer heard Fran's voice.

"How are you, Fran? I'm doing okay. I still haven't got a job but trying to find myself. Don't know what I want to do yet. May go into teaching like you."

"I thought I lost you for a second there, Athena. I know I was going on for a long time. I might have put you to sleep. Don't worry you will find something that you like to do. How did you know I'm a teacher?"

"No chance of that, Fran. It's so good to hear your voice. I spoke with Lacy last night, or I should say, this morning. She is doing well and told me you are a teacher."

"Yes, I love it! I am crazy about kids! They are so much fun to teach. I love watching their little faces when I explain something new to them. They light up!"

"That's wonderful, Fran. I hope one day to find something I love to do too.

"Of course you will. Are you married yet, Athena?"

"No, but found a nice guy. In fact, you probably remember him from college – Justin, the hunky one."

"Ooh, yes. I remember the hunk man himself. All the girls loved him. You never really looked his way back then. How come?"

"Well, I didn't think I stood a chance with all the girls that hung around him, especially the cheerleaders."

"Oh God, they were disgusting! They wouldn't leave him alone for a minute."

"That's funny, Fran. Lacy said the same thing."

"Did she? I guess we think alike! Well, tell me more about the hunk man."

"There really isn't much to tell yet. We just went on a quick coffee date after my writing class."

"Writing class? Aren't you tired of taking classes?"

"Right, Lacy said that too. Yep, I am. But my mother pushed me into taking it. I'm glad I did though. I wouldn't have run into Justin if I hadn't."

"Oh, I see. You saw him there and went out for coffee afterwards. Did you click together after all this time?"

"Yes, surprisingly we did. He was a gentleman and even opened the door of the car for me. He kissed my hand when he brought me to my door too. That was nice."

"Kissed your hand? Wow, that's nice for a change. No groping or tongues involved there!"

"Right, none involved. You are too funny, Fran. I've missed you. You said you had something to tell me. What have you been up to?"

"Well, besides teaching I have been dating a great guy for two years now. He asked me to marry him. We set our date for late fall. That brings me to ask you. Will you be my maid of honor?"

"Oh my! I would love to, Fran. Thank you so much. I'm sorry it's been so long that we lost touch with one another. Let's not let that happen again. In fact, I want to set a date for you, Lacy and me to go out for dinner. What night is good for you?"

"Great! I would love that. I will tell my fiancé, Jarred that I need to set aside one night to be with my friends. I think he can do without me for one night."

"Okay, as long as it's okay with him. After all, he will have you all to himself soon enough. We need to keep close to our girlfriends."

"You betcha. Friends matter and are important. We can't go through life without them."

"What night can you spare, Fran?"

"Let's see. I have my calendar on the wall. I am so forgetful. I need reminders of what I am doing every day. Things are going to get crazy when we get closer to the wedding date. How about Friday. That's only two days away."

"Sounds good to me. I'll call Lacy and see if she can do that night too. I'll text you with 'okay' or not."

"Great. Well, I've got to go. It's been super talking to you again, Athena. Can't wait to see you both on Friday. Love you lots, girlfriend."

"Same here, Fran. Love you back."

Athena sat back on her couch and sighed happily. She could get used to being this happy or should she say snorky feeling. She giggled like a schoolgirl. It felt so good to talk to her friends. Now all she needed to do was connect with Justin again. She crossed her fingers that he would call soon.

Her phone rang again and she looked at the screen. It was her mother again. Did she really need to talk to her again? What else did she need to know about her writing class?

Athena sighed as she accepted the call. "Hi Mom. How are you?"

"Athena, are you okay? You sound so tired."

"No, I'm fine. I slept plenty last night."

Her mother waited another minute to hear more about her sleeping habits. "Did you have any nightmares?"

"No, Mom. I did not dream last night. In fact, I haven't been dreaming much lately. I feel better and rested, so you don't have to worry about me. Okay?" Athena didn't want to get into explaining about her dream.

"Okay, dear. Your father wanted me to check up on you. We worry about you, you know."

"Yes, mother, I know you both do. I am not a little child anymore. There is no need to worry yourself about me. I've got to go. I have some cleaning to do around here. Talk to you tomorrow."

"Okay, honey. Love you. Take care. Talk to you soon."

"Yes, love you too."

Athena ended the call and sighed heavily. I can't believe they won't let me have any space. I don't think I can take this. I need to find someone to spend time with. I'll call Lacy and set the date for Friday. I'll really need to get out and away.

Before Athena could make the call she received another call. This one was the much hoped for one – Justin.

"Hello."

"Athena? It's Justin. I had a difficult time tracking you down but I finally found you. How have you been? I really want to see you again."

Athena sighed but this time in a good way. "Hi Justin. It's good to hear from you. I would love to see you again too. I had a nice time the other night."

"Great! How about Friday?"

"Oh. That is the only night I am busy with my girlfriends. I haven't seen them in a long time. I'm sorry. Can we do it the following night?"

There was silence on the other end of the phone as Athena waited for Justin's response.

"If tomorrow is not good for you, Justin, I can try to change it with my friends."

"Oh no, I wouldn't ask that of you. Of course, Saturday will be perfect. Do you want to try the new Italian restaurant, Napolitano's, downtown? I heard it's excellent."

"Yes, yes, that would be great. Thank you for understanding. I'm sorry about Friday."

"Athena, you don't need to apologize. I think it's wonderful that you spend time with your girlfriends. You need that. Well, I won't keep you. I look forward to seeing you on Saturday. I'll pick you up at 6:30 pm. Okay? See you then."

"Okay. See you then, Justin. Thank you. I look forward to it too."

Athena danced around as soon as she ended the call. She couldn't believe Justin had called her. She wondered how he had obtained her number. How did he do that?

But wait a minute, he did drop me off after coffee recently. I guess he must have found my phone number by looking up my address.

Her previous feeling of contentment turned to apprehension. She would have to find out more about this man. How well did she know him? They had just had one date and she did most of the talking. Well, that would have to change. She needed to know more about him. Suddenly she was nervous about seeing him Saturday night. She would have some questions for Justin.

CHAPTER FIVE

The girls met at a local place called The Eatery that had a jukebox and a dance floor. It was a fun place to go that had delicious burgers and waffle fries.

Fran and Lacy were there first and jumped up from their booth when they saw Athena coming through the doorway. The three acted like they were kids again as they hugged and kissed and exclaimed how happy they were to be together again.

"It's so good to see you both," Athena exclaimed as she continued to walk arm in arm with her friends to the booth.

"I can't believe we waited so long to get together. I guess our lives became busy and we went in separate directions," Lacy explained.

Fran added, "Yep, I guess that's what happens after you graduate. You never see some of your fellow graduates ever again. I'm glad you contacted us, Athena. I'm sorry I neglected to keep in touch."

"Me too, Athena. I've really missed you both," Lacy gushed as she signaled for the waitress to come to take their order. "Let's get a bottle of wine. I hope you are drinking something better these days than the sweet stuff, girls."

"Of course. I wasn't the one to start drinking that stuff. It was cheap though. Let's get something good but not too expensive," Athena announced with a smirk.

They looked over the wine list and picked one that was in the mid-range. When their glasses were filled they made a toast and sighed.

"Well, this is perfect, girls! A girls' night out is just what I needed." Athena clinked glasses with her friends and was suddenly quiet.

"Hey, what's up, Athena. Why are you looking so glum?" Lacy probed.

"Did Justin not call you yet?" Fran inquired as she exchanged worried looks with Lacy.

"No, I mean yes, he did."

"Well, that's great, Athena! So what's the problem?"

Athena put her glass down, met her friends eyes and said, "It's okay. There isn't a problem. Well, I…I'm a little nervous about how he suddenly could get my phone number without even asking me. Don't you think that's strange?"

"Hmm, well, not really, Athena. I think Justin really likes you and went out of his way to find your number. He's a clever guy." Lacy smiled reassuringly.

"Right! You said he was a lawyer? Well, that explains everything. They have ways to find people, you know," Fran added with a wink.

"I guess so."

"Come on, Athena. Snap out of it. Did he ask you out again?" Lacy looked closely at Athena's troubled face.

"Yes, he did. In fact, he wanted to go out tonight but I told him I was busy with my friends."

"Really? You could have changed our night out to another night."

"I know, Fran. I offered to do that but he refused and suggested going out tomorrow night instead."

"That's great! So what are you so upset over? You were excited about being out with him when I last spoke with you. What changed that?" Fran asked, confusion spreading across her face.

Athena explained that she had a funny feeling that something wasn't quite right.

"Stop it right now, Athena. Get out of this maudlin mood and let's have a good time. We need to do some serious catching up and partying here," Lacy announced as she clinked glasses once again with Fran then Athena.

Athena looked up and smiled. You're right. Sorry. I don't know what gets into me sometimes. I guess it's my mother. She called me twice today. I need to get away from her. Having this night out with you and a date tomorrow is just what the doctor ordered."

"That's better, my friend," Fran stated with a wide grin.

Lacy headed over to the jukebox and chose one of her favorite songs. Once the song began she grabbed the girls and pulled them onto the empty dance floor. They swayed and bounced around as they got into the music. Before long they were having a great time and feeling like they were back at college.

The waitress came over and poured the rest of the wine for the girls. When the song ended they went back to their booth and drank some more wine feeling mellow and happy.

"Hey, I'm starving! Let's order some burgers and fries," Fran announced.

"Sounds good to me," Lacy agreed.

Athena sipped her wine and was a million miles away again.

"Wake up, girlfriend. Did you hear what we just said?" Fran poked Athena to get her attention.

"Oh, sorry. I guess my mind was wandering again. Yes, I would love a burger and waffle fries. They are delicious here."

Lacy waved at the waitress to say they were ready to order.

Half an hour later they were devouring juicy burgers and crispy waffle fries to die for drenched in ketchup.

"These are incredible, Athena. So glad you led us to this place. It's new, isn't it? I didn't even know it was here," Fran stated in between bites and wiping away the meat juice from her lips.

"You're welcome! I love this place. I've been here a couple of times with my parents since it opened up. You can imagine how exciting it was with them," Athena rolled her eyes.

"What's up with your parents? Are they still overprotective of you? Why don't they give you some space?" Lacy inquired with a tilt of her head.

Athena shrugged her shoulders. "I wish I knew. They never give me a breather. I avoid going over there and don't share anything with them. My dad always asks who I am seeing each time. I always tell him no one special. I won't share my date with Justin with them."

"Didn't you go out with a guy in college that disappeared all of a sudden? What was his name?" Lacy asked.

"Yes. That was Brian. We only dated for a month and then he stopped calling me. I never heard from him again."

"Hmm, that's strange. You liked him a lot, didn't you, Athena?" Lacy knitted her brows as she observed Athena.

"Well, he was a nice guy and a gentleman. Not like some of the guys back then who were pigs."

"Yes, I remember some of them well," Fran guffawed.

The girls chatted more about some of their dates in college who were losers and had many chuckles. The night passed by quickly as they became once again close friends erasing all the distance between them since graduation.

Athena yawned and looked at her friends guiltily. "Sorry, ladies. I guess I have had enough wine. It's making me sleepy. Maybe it's time to call it a night. It's been so much fun seeing you both. Let's make this a regular thing to do at least once a month. What do you think?"

Both Fran and Lacy piped up together, "Great! Perfect! Take out your calendars, ladies!"

They looked over some dates and came to a consensus about their next night out.

Fran was the first to ask, "Athena, remember you need to call us and let us know about your date with Justin and how it goes. Right?"

"Hmm, do I have to tell all?" Athena giggled.

"You bet you do! We want every minute detail," Lacy added with a chuckle.

"Well, I'll think about it," Athena smiled and pulled out her wallet to pay her share when the waitress handed out their bills.

The ladies shared a taxi and said their goodbyes after promising to keep in touch.

CHAPTER SIX

Athena was excited and anxious at the same time the following day, anticipating seeing Justin again. She didn't think the time would ever come for their date to begin. She kept herself busy around the apartment and even wrote a couple of chapters in a new book she had started a few months ago. Suddenly her motivation was there.

Time passed once she had gotten into her story. She looked at the clock in her kitchen and realized that it was already 5:30. Justin was coming at 6:30. Athena rushed back to her bedroom and scanned through her closet for an outfit. This was the time that she didn't like anything she had there. Now what was she going to do? She had to find something.

She pulled out different outfits and held them against her in front of her full length mirror. It was now almost 6:00. She had to make a decision and make it quickly or she wouldn't be ready for him.

She finally decided on a black sheath dress with a boat neck. She chose a sparkly necklace and hoop earrings along with her black mid-heels. She looked over her makeup and applied a minimal amount to cover any imperfections and added some blush and eye shadow and liner ending with a pretty pink lipstick. She brushed her hair and pinned up the sides so that they accentuated her high cheekbones. She stepped back and looked herself over, satisfied that she would pass inspection with her mother if she was here.

Why did she even think that way? It wasn't her mother's call to decide what she wore or how she looked on a date.

Athena sighed and headed back to the living room to wait for Justin. She grabbed her purse and threw a few needed items into it and a light sweater in case it got cooler later. She didn't know where he was taking her. He hadn't told her. She only hoped she wasn't overdressed.

As she was running all the scenarios over in her head about what her mother thought or why it mattered so much to her, the doorbell rang.

She peeked into the mirror in the hall to recheck her appearance before answering the door. When she opened it there stood the handsomest man she had ever seen. She didn't realize Justin was talking to her at first because she was holding her breath and couldn't speak.

"Hello, Athena. You look lovely."

"Oh, hi Justin. Thank you. You look …umm…nice too."

Justin smiled and reached out his hand to Athena. She picked up her purse and sweater on the chair near the door and took his hand as she followed him out to his car.

Justin looked at Athena and couldn't believe how beautiful she was. He opened the passenger door and got her seated before going to the driver side.

"Are you okay, Athena? You're so quiet."

"Yes, I'm fine, Justin. I…I…umm…just fine. Where are we going?"

"Well, I did mention to you the new Italian place. Do you remember me saying that? If that isn't good, we can go somewhere else."

"Oh, I'm sorry. I did forget you mentioned that. The Italian restaurant is perfect. I don't know where my head is. I guess I am becoming forgetful."

"No problem, Athena. You must have had a good time last night with your friends. Was it too much fun and drink for you?" Justin chuckled.

"Well, that must be it. Yes, we did have a little too much wine to drink but had a real good time," Athena smiled thinking over last night's dancing and non-stop talking with her friends.

Justin looked over at Athena and said with a smirk, "Yes, I can see you had a great time. You are beaming."

"Am I? I didn't realize I was. Well, it had been a couple of years since I had spoken to my friends. It was really nice to catch up with them."

"I bet it was. I know what you mean. I haven't seen some of my college friends in a couple of years either. I've been too busy working."

"Maybe you should call them and catch up too. It could do you wonders like it did for me. You work too hard and need to have some fun once in a while."

"I guess you're right but I had something else in mind, Athena."

"What?"

"I plan to spend a lot of time with you."

Athena glanced over at Justin and saw the beautiful smile on his face.

"Is that okay with you?"

"Yes, umm…I would like that too." Athena could feel her face flushing with heat.

"You aren't blushing, are you, Athena?" Justin chuckled.

"Well, I…maybe. I didn't expect you to say that."

"Well, if you must know, I didn't expect I would say that either. But I really like you, Athena, and want to spend a lot more time with you. Is that okay?"

Athena's face was deeply flushed and she stammered, "Of course, Justin. I…I would like that too."

"Well, now that that is settled, let's go eat! We're here!"

Before Athena could say anything else, Justin opened her door and offered his hand to help her out of the car.

"Thank you."

"No problem, my lady."

With Justin's steady gaze on Athena, he led her into the restaurant and gave his name to the hostess at the reservation desk.

They were seated immediately and a bottle of Chianti was already on the table. The wine steward poured wine into their glasses and stepped back.

"Thank you. We would like to look over the menu and sample the wine for a little bit."

"No problem, Sir. I will send over your server when you let me know you are ready to order."

Justin nodded and said, "Thank you."

"Well, they must know you here. There was a bottle of Chianti on the table ready."

"When I made the reservations I asked them to do that. I thought you might like it to go with our meal."

"Yes, I love red wine, Chianti and others. They do go perfectly with Italian food."

"I've been here a couple of times and love the chicken or veal parmigiana, and the mussels Italiano."

"Those all sound delicious to me. Okay, let's begin with an order of mussels. Okay?"

"Sure. Sounds good to me. My stomach is growling already."

"Oh, is that what I just heard?" Justin laughed as he waved at the server to come over.

"Do you know what you would like to have for your meal?"

"Yes! I would love the chicken parmigiana."

The server asked, "What kind of pasta would you like, Miss? We have linguine, fettuccine, farfalle, and penne."

Athena thought over the choices and answered, "I would like fettuccine."

A salad comes with your meal, Miss. What kind of dressing do you prefer?

"House Italian would be fine."

"And you, Sir?"

Justin asked for the mussels' appetizer and chose veal parmigiana with penne and salad with creamy Italian for his meal. He waited for the waiter to leave before picking up his glass and making a toast to Athena.

"Here's to you, Athena. I'm blessed to see you again. It was meant to be that we would run into each other at the class."

"Yes, I guess so, Justin. I was so surprised to see you too."

"You don't sound too happy, Athena. Is everything all right? Did I say something to upset you?"

"No...no you didn't, Justin. I was thinking about..."

"What? What were you thinking about, Athena?" He asked softly.

Justin reached across the table and gently took Athena's hand. He stroked it and waited to hear what she had to say.

"I...I was wondering, Justin, how you got my phone number. I didn't give it to you nor did you ask for it."

"Yes, I neglected to ask you but I found it by looking online. You do realize that you can obtain just about anyone's information online?"

"I guess so. I never did that."

"Athena, dear, please don't be upset. I hate to see you like this. Maybe it's time to get another bear claw or something else for your sweet tooth."

A smile crept across Athena's lips as she met Justin's steady gaze. "Ah, I see that is the secret to your heart."

The waiter appeared suddenly with their mussels' appetizer.

They didn't wait long before they devoured them all and sat back and sighed.

"That was absolutely delicious, Justin. Wow, I should tell my friends about this place. I know they will love it too."

"Yes, I'm sure they would. I'm so happy that you enjoyed the mussels. I've had them in other places but this is the best."

"I agree," Athena smiled as she dabbed her lips with her napkin.

Before another word could be said, the waiter whisked away their dishes and returned shortly thereafter with their meals. He promptly set each plate in front of them and stepped away. He asked before leaving if there was anything else they would need.

"Thank you, Sir. I think we are good for now, right Athena?"

"Yes, I'm fine." Her smile now reached her eyes as she looked at Justin.

They were quiet as they enjoyed their meals and sipped Chianti.

Athena felt her anxiety dissipate and then disappear completely as she finished off her second glass of wine.

Justin watched her in silence and poured her another glass from a second bottle he had asked the waiter to bring when he noticed they were finished with the first one.

"How's your chicken parmigiana, Athena?"

"Oh, it's absolutely delicious! I will have to come here more often."

"Well, I take that as a chance for another date," Justin chuckled.

"Oh my! I didn't mean that to come out like that. So sorry. I wasn't asking for another date."

"I wish you were because I planned to ask you out at the end of the night for another one."

"I see. Okay. I'll wait to give you my answer at that time." Athena met his gaze with a satisfied smile on her face.

Justin smiled back, nodded as he finished his veal, and poured more wine in both of their glasses.

Athena didn't get her hand over her glass in time to stop him. Instead she picked up her glass and toasted him with a clink of her glass.

"What do you think? Are you ready for something sweet?"

"Hmm, that sounds good. What do they have for desserts here?"

"I'll get our waiter and find out." Justin waved at their waiter and he hurriedly came over with dessert menus.

"We would love some dessert and coffees."

"Okay. What kind of coffee would you like?"

Athena spoke up first and said "Decaf, cream no sugar."

"And you, Sir?"

"I'll have regular coffee, cream and one sugar, please. You can get our coffees as we peruse the desserts."

"Certainly, Sir. Be right back."

Athena looked over the menu and smiled as she saw some of her favorites on it – cannoli, strawberry shortcake, Crème Brule and brownie sundae.

"Have you made a decision yet, Athena?" Justin couldn't help watching her face as it lit up with delight over the choices.

"Well, I like them all but I think I would like to try their strawberry shortcake."

"Hmm, that sounds good."

The waiter returned with their coffees and looked at Justin for his choice.

"We will each have a strawberry shortcake."

"Good choice, Sir. You won't find a better shortcake anywhere in town," he smiled and bowed away.

Athena couldn't control her amusement over the waiter and his solicitous behavior.

Justin joined her in laughing over how hard this man was trying to get a good tip.

"He has no worries. I planned on giving him a generous tip. But it's nice to see him trying so hard to please us. I like that."

"Maybe you wouldn't feel so generous if he hadn't tried this hard."

"You're right, Athena. I think he really earned his money tonight," he chuckled.

Athena watched his face as his eyes crinkled when he laughed and his whole persona took on an aura of light. She blinked a couple of times to make sure she wasn't imagining this.

They talked about everything, movies, their favorite things, and what they have been doing since graduation. They were slowly getting to know one another better and enjoying every minute of it.

The night flew by and it was soon time to leave. The waiter thanked Justin profusely for his generosity and invited him back again real soon.

Justin laughed, winked at Athena, and said they would definitely be back.

CHAPTER SEVEN

The ride home was quiet and peaceful as they both listened to some soft rock on the radio.

Athena felt a warm feeling all over her most likely from all the wine she had consumed. She smiled to herself and looked over at Justin's profile. He was such a handsome man, so kind and caring. She couldn't believe how lucky she was that he was actually interested in her.

Before long, they had arrived at her apartment and she realized that she didn't want to leave him. She heard a sigh escape her lips and Justin looked at her and smiled.

"I had a lovely time, Justin. Thank you. The restaurant was perfect in every way."

"You're welcome, my dear. Do you remember that I said I was going to ask you out again?"

"Umm, yes. I did."

"Well, what do you say we do this again next Saturday? But this time we try the Seafood Catch across town. I've tried it already with some of my colleagues and it's excellent."

"Sounds good."

"Oh, I forgot to ask if you like seafood."

"Yes, definitely. I love it. In fact, just about every fish and shellfish there is."

"Thank goodness. I almost blew it, didn't I?"

"Not at all, Justin. I'm sure I would have found something to order even if I didn't like fish."

"Phew! Okay, let's make it the same time. That was good for you, right?"

"Yes, it was perfect. Everything was perfect tonight. I can't thank you enough for such a lovely evening."

"Let me walk you to the door. Don't move. I will get the door."

Athena smiled contentedly as she waited for this man to do his thing in such a gallant way.

He walked her to the door and looked into her eyes and smiled.

Athena smiled back and waited to see if he would kiss her. She even leaned in a little to make it easier for him.

Justin complied and leaned in closer. Their lips met softly at first then more firmly. She felt his tongue pushing against her lips and she invited it in and shared hers in kind.

She felt a swoon coming on as her knees became weak and she held onto his shoulders and pushed herself into his chest to get a better grip on him.

He complied and pulled her into his muscular chest and the kiss became deeper. He let out a low rumbling sound as he continued to kiss her and didn't let go.

Athena sighed and held on for dear life. She thought she was going to pass out. This was their first kiss and it was going on and on. How much more could she take?

Just as she thought she couldn't stop the warm feeling flooding deep inside her and into her limbs, she felt him lightly step back. Her toes were tingling with desire.

Athena couldn't stop herself as he caught her and hugged her against him. Justin gripped her before she fell forward.

This was almost as good as the kiss, she thought.

"I think I should let you go. You're tired, I'm sure, and we both had too much to drink. I had a wonderful evening also, Athena. Sleep well. I look forward to our next date."

"Yes, I think you are right. Thank you again, Justin. I look forward to next weekend too. Good night."

Justin leaned in and kissed her lips one more time but ever so lightly and stepped away.

Athena found herself sighing again as she smiled, turned to unlock her door and stepped across the threshold clearly not feeling too steady.

"Are you okay, Athena?" Justin asked as he waited for her to turn and then close the door.

"Yes, I'm fine. Thank you. Good night."

"Good night, my lovely Athena, until next weekend."

She watched him from her front window as he pulled away from the curb until she couldn't see him anymore.

She dropped her sweater and purse on the chair and floated on air through the living room to her bedroom. She pulled off her clothes and picked out a nightgown and dropped it over her head. She went into the bathroom and somehow brushed her teeth.

The next thing she remembered was falling onto her bed until she woke up with another nightmare.

***

She saw herself in a car and someone was driving but she couldn't turn her head to look at who it was. They were traveling too fast and swerving all over the road. The rain was coming down in buckets and the tires were hydroplaning.

She heard a screech of brakes as the tires left the road and the car flew into the air. She screamed and watched as the ground came closer.

The next minute she was sitting up in bed and trembling with fright and cold. She looked around and was confused. What just happened and why? Where was Justin? Is this going to happen? Is she seeing the future again?

Athena looked at her alarm clock. It was only four o'clock, much too early to get up. She laid down again and tried to think of happy thoughts. She tossed and turned and finally fell asleep again.

She was soon into the same dream but this time her father was driving. He looked at her and laughed as he pressed the gas pedal and increased the speed. He swerved back and forth on the road and kept laughing as the car left the pavement and catapulted into the air.

Athena screamed and thrashed around in bed until she finally woke up. She shivered and rubbed her arms that felt ice cold.

What was going on here? Now she saw her father driving. What did this mean? Is her father going to die? Will she die with him?

She wished she could talk to her grandmother Grace. She was living in Europe and had been for the last twenty years. Her mother, Carla, sent her grandmother away. She did not want her to influence Athena in any way. After all, Gramma was clairvoyant and known to predict things from the future. Carla was afraid that Athena inherited this gene to do these things.

Athena remembered spending time with her grandmother and how much fun they had playing cards, board games, talking and just dancing around. She could always say anything to Gramma Grace. She loved her more than she loved her parents, who didn't listen to her or play with her when she was a child.

The day that Gramma Grace left, five-year-old Athena cried for hours, broken hearted. She kept asking her mother, "Why did Gramma leave and when is she coming back?"

Her mother kept saying, "It was for the best, Athena. Now she can't teach you what you shouldn't know."

"What shouldn't I know, Mom? What? Please tell me!"

Her mother would ignore her and walk away without answering.

Athena learned to make up play times with her grandmother and pulled out her cards and board games and pretended that Gramma Grace was there playing with her.

One day when she was playing cards, the cards she had placed across from her for her grandmother actually moved. She thought she was seeing things but they moved again. She reached across and touched them. They were warm as if someone was holding them.

Athena whispered, "Gramma Grace, are you there?"

It was as if her grandmother was in the room with her. She heard her laugh, reached across, touched the cards and felt her presence there.

From then on, Athena spent many hours playing with her Gramma and talking to her. She could hear her grandmother's voice in her head teaching her how to do the things that her mother didn't want Athena to learn.

Athena was still too young to understand some of what her grandmother told her that she could do. Gramma Grace said time will tell and she will learn more.

She was just happy to have her grandmother with her, even if it was only in her head.

As she got older, Athena no longer played or talked to her grandmother. She didn't feel the need any more. Her grandmother's voice was becoming fainter. Athena still thought about her often but was becoming busier in her life with school and stuff that teenagers did.

Her parents kept a close watch over her. They never questioned her about her playtimes when she was younger. But she caught her mother watching her as she passed by her room on many occasions.

After her first college boyfriend, Brian, disappeared she wished she could talk to her grandmother again but there was no longer a connection. She wondered if something had happened to her.

CHAPTER EIGHT

Back to Present Time

Athena laid back on her pillow in the hospital bed and sighed as she looked at Dr. Jasper. He nodded and said, "It's okay, Athena. You told me quite a bit about your life and your parents. I think you are doing well and can get back home soon and recuperate. I will check with Dr. Nettles."

The door to her room opened and in came Dr. Nettles. He wore a wide smile that crinkled his eyes.

"Well, our lovely patient is awake. How are you feeling today, Athena?" Dr. Nettles inquired as he exchanged nods with Dr. Jasper.

Athena stated once again, "I'm confused," Dr. Nettles. "I don't understand what happened to Justin. What's going on here?"

"Athena, dear, we will work it all out. Don't you worry, okay? Did you have a nice visit with Dr. Jasper?"

"Yes, we have been talking about my parents and my life so far."

"That's good. I think it's time to get you back home. Don't you think so too, Dr. Jasper?"

"Yes, most definitely. I was just stating that fact before you walked in."

"Ah, yes. I'm glad we agree, Dr. Jasper. So, what do you think, Athena? Are you ready to go home?"

"Oh, yes! I want to get out of this bed. When can I leave?"

"Well, I need to sign off at the desk and write some orders for you to take it easy for a little while longer. Then you should be able to leave later today or first thing in the morning."

"Not in the morning, please. I'm ready now," Athena stated emphatically.

"Okay, let me see what I can do." Turning to Dr. Jasper, he said softly, "Let's have a little talk, Nick. See you at the desk."

Dr. Jasper nodded and said to Athena, "Well, it looks like you will be going home soon. I'll leave my orders at the desk for you to call my office after you get home. I would like to see you again in about two weeks. Okay?"

Athena nodded and sighed. "Okay."

***

Dr. Jasper and Dr. Nettles stopped by the desk and finished writing up Athena's release orders along with their recommendations.

"Nick, what did you learn about Athena?"

"She told me about her background, her relationship with her parents, Justin, and her grandmother Grace."

"Ah, yes, grandmother Grace. She is quite an extraordinary person."

"In what way, Ash? I know Athena mentioned communicating with her through her mind. I thought that was only because she needed her. That was Athena's way of surviving without this person who she loved and loved her back unconditionally."

"Yes, that too. But what you have to understand is Grace is not an ordinary person. She has powers that I have witnessed but still don't understand. The Stones ostracized Grace to keep her away from their daughter. They did not want their Athena to become like her grandmother."

"Do you think that Athena has powers like her grandmother?"

"Yes, I believe she does. She has been having nightmares since she was young. She sees things before they happen."

"Wait a minute. Do you mean she had dreamed of this accident before it happened? What about Justin? Why wasn't he in the car like she dreamed?"

"That is a good question. I don't understand that either, Nick. But that is up to you to figure out. Psychiatry is your field of study, not mine."

"But, Nick. This is not psychiatry, this is a paranormal phenomenon. This is not in my field of study."

"Well, it's closer to yours than it is to mine," Ash chuckled.

"Maybe just a little," Nick laughed and slapped Dr. Nettles on the back. "I'll do what I can to figure it all out."

"That's my boy. I knew I could count on you to do that. Athena is in need of your help. She is lost and confused and needs your direction. Please do all that you can."

"I will, Ash. I will do my best."

***

Athena got up from the bed slowly and looked around for her clothes. The nurse came in at that moment and handed Athena a bag with her belongings. She guided her to the bathroom to change and handed her a toothbrush and toothpaste.

When the two doctors returned to her room, Athena was dressed and ready to leave. Her clothes were a little crumpled and torn from her accident but would have to do until she could get home and change.

"Ahh, Athena. Nice to see you are ready and able to leave. Did you call anyone to pick you up?"

"No, I didn't. I planned on taking a taxi."

"That won't do, Athena," Dr. Nettles announced with a look of concern.

"Oh no, Dr. Nettles. I will not call my parents. You know how they are. They will drive me crazy. They will insist on me staying with them so they can hover over me. I promise to call them when I get home."

Dr. Jasper cleared his throat to get attention, "Wait a minute, I'm ready to leave now. Let me take Athena home, Dr. Nettles. It's no problem at all."

"Are you sure? I can take her after I finish up my rounds within the hour."

"Really, doctors? I don't need anyone to take me home. I can handle that myself. There is no need to disrupt either of your plans."

"Athena, you would not be disrupting my plans. I don't have any. I was going home to an empty house and a TV dinner, I hate to admit."

"Hmm, what kind of TV dinner, doctor?" Athena asked, stifling a giggle.

"Well, I haven't yet decided," Dr. Jasper replied with a smirk. "I have quite a full freezer of all kinds."

Dr. Nettles smiled as he listened to their interchange. "Are you ready to leave, Athena?"

"Yes, I'm ready, Dr. Nettles. Here are your orders. I want to see you in a couple of weeks, unless you have any problems sooner than that."

"Thank you, Dr. Nettles. I'll call to make an appointment. I promise."

"I know you will, Athena. Now, go with Dr. Jasper and rest until you feel strong enough to do your everyday things. For goodness sake, young lady, eat better too."

"Okay, I plan to eat something better than a TV dinner, that's for sure." She exchanged smiles with Dr. Jasper.

Dr. Nettles shook hands with Dr. Jasper and whispered. "She's in your capable hands, Nick. Thanks."

"No problem, Ash." Dr. Jasper turned toward Athena and said, "This way, Athena."

The ride to her house was quiet. Neither one of them had anything to say at first.

Athena was the first to break the silence. "Dr. Jasper, I appreciate this. You really didn't have to take me home. I am quite capable of taking care of myself."

"I know you are. But it made Dr. Nettles feel better. He worries about you like a father."

"Yes, I know. I think of him as a father sometimes too. He is more of a father to me than my own…" Athena stopped when she felt tears welling.

Dr. Jasper snuck a peek at her and noticed the tears threatening to fall. He didn't say anything and let her gather herself. He waited until she was calm again and asked, "What do you want to have for lunch or early dinner?"

Athena glanced at him and smiled. "I thought you were planning to have a TV dinner, doctor?"

"Well, I would have if I didn't have a better idea."

"Hmm, I see. What do you have in mind, doctor?"

"I asked you first, Athena. It's your choice. I am doing what Dr. Nettles ordered, to make sure you eat well."

"Okay, I'm up for some subs. There's a sub shop not far from my house. They have delicious Italian subs, cutlets, and one of my favorites, pastrami with plenty of spicy mustard!"

"Sounds good to me. Give me directions."

Athena told him he was almost there. "Turn here, doc, and it is around the corner. Take the next right."

"Tucker's Subs?"

"Yep! That's it! Do you want me to go in and order?"

"Absolutely not, young lady. I am a gentleman. It would be my pleasure to get you a pastrami sub with plenty of spicy mustard. My preference is that

Italian sub you mentioned. My mouth is salivating now as I think about it. Stay right here and I'll be back shortly."

Athena sat back and sighed. She liked being taken care of by this gentleman. She watched him as he entered the shop and noticed that he was in excellent shape and quite good looking.

She suddenly felt shy when he came back. She couldn't believe what she was thinking. She actually felt attracted to him. It must be her mind. She wasn't quite right yet. She needed to find Justin and couldn't be thinking of another man. What was wrong with her?

"Smells good, huh? You said your apartment is around the corner. Which direction?"

"Take a left here. It's up ahead, the blue one with the black shutters."

Athena jumped out of the car before Dr. Jasper could open her door. She was feeling uncomfortable about her thoughts. She raced up the front stairs and unlocked her door leaving it open for him.

"Well, you must be starving. You were in a hurry to get inside," Dr. Jasper stated with a frown.

"Sorry. I guess I'm just glad to be home."

"Where do you want to eat, kitchen table or island?"

"Island is okay with me. What would you like to drink, doctor?"

"Water is fine," he replied as he removed their sandwiches and put them on the plates Athena had placed on the island. "Looks delicious! I can't wait to try mine," he gestured and prepared to lift up his sandwich to take a bite. "But I should first wash my hands." He went over to the sink and soaped up. He kept his eyes on Athena as she walked by him and sat down to eat.

"How is it? Good as I said?" Athena waited until the doctor had taken a couple of bites.

"Oh, much better. I will have to visit this place again. It's much better than my TV dinners, even if I have to come from across town to get a sub."

"Yes, it is," Athena relaxed and chuckled as she bit into her sub and audibly sighed.

"I guess yours is as good from your deep sigh of pleasure."

"Most definitely, yes!" Athena smiled with her mouth full trying to keep the food in her mouth at the same time as the mustard dripped onto her lips.

After they had finished their lunch, Athena was feeling uncomfortable and said, "I don't want to keep you, Dr. Jasper."

"No problem. I'm leaving, Athena. Thank you for suggesting Tucker's. It was excellent. I'm feeling quite sated. Well, take care. Don't forget to call my office for an appointment in two weeks."

"Thank you for the sub. I appreciate that. I promise to call. Thank you for the ride too."

Dr. Jasper nodded, smiled, and looked deep into Athena's beautiful eyes that had now changed to green.

"My pleasure, Athena. Look forward to seeing you in my office in two weeks. If you need me before that time, don't hesitate to call."

"Okay, thank you. I will." Athena met his blue eyes and felt herself blushing as she walked him to the door.

He looked up, waved and pulled away from the curb. She stepped back from the window and returned to the kitchen to clean up. Her thoughts were still on his blue eyes that had looked at her so deeply.

CHAPTER NINE

After Dr. Jasper left, Athena pulled out her playing cards that she had kept from her childhood. They were quite tattered but still somewhat usable. She whispered, "Gramma Grace, are you there?"

She waited for several minutes after she dealt the cards and placed the rest of the deck on the kitchen table. She sighed and tried to keep the tears at bay.

"Gramma Grace, I need you. Can you hear me?"

A breeze blew across the table and the cards scattered. Athena looked around, collected the cards and called out, "Is that you, Gramma Grace?"

She felt a touch on her cheek and jumped. Athena whispered, "I know you are here, Gramma Grace. I can feel you in the room and you just touched my cheek."

"Yes, dear. I can hear you. I've been thinking about you too. Are you doing better since the accident?"

"How did you know about it?"

"I've been watching you from afar. Remember, I can see things into the future. So can you. Have you figured that out yet?"

"Yes, I've been having nightmares about an accident. Then it happened but I was alone. I can't find Justin. Do you know where he is? No one will tell me."

"Child, don't worry about that. I think you are getting ahead of yourself. Sometimes this power that we have is confusing. We see things that are not really there yet. We think that they have happened when something similar happens."

"What do you mean, Gramma Grace? I don't understand."

"Well, you met this young man, Justin, right? You went out to dinner with him but then you skipped to the accident. What happened in between? Do you remember how you came to be in the car?"

"No, I just remember feeling happy and that he had asked me to marry him. Then we went for a ride in his car and then…"

"Did that really happen? Are you sure?"

"No, not really. But I was in a car accident and in the hospital for a month or at least that's what the doctors told me."

"Yes, you were. Think about this. Where is your ring, Athena?"

"I don't know. I don't have one. Maybe you are right, Gramma. It never happened like I thought. But where was I going in such a hurry that I got into an accident?"

"I think I need to come visit you in person. It is too difficult to talk to you this way. I miss you, honey."

"Yes, please come. I won't tell Mom about you visiting."

"Don't worry about her. It's time that she and I have a long talk. She lets that husband of hers control everything in her life, even you. I don't want to discuss this now, Athena, dear. I will call you when I can come. Okay? Will you be able to pick me up at the airport?"

"Yes, most definitely, Gramma Grace. Let me know when and I will be there. I can't wait to see you again. I've missed you too."

"Thank you, dear. We will fix all of this for you as soon as I can get there. Don't worry. It will all work out. Take care, child. I love you."

"I love you, too, Gramma Grace. See you soon!"

***

Athena was feeling more relaxed since she had spoken long distance with her grandmother. Gramma Grace always had the answers to her problems and would somehow help her understand what was happening to her.

She tried to think back over the years about her father's strange behavior and how her mother appeared to be afraid of him. Athena did what she was told to do and never tested her father's temper or her mother's patience. She knew there was something wrong between them. They never showed any affection toward one another or to her. She was usually in her own world most of the time or spending time with her Gramma Grace in person or in virtual time, so it didn't affect her much. Her grandmother gave her all the love and attention she would ever need.

What would she have done without her grandmother's love? She might have turned out like her parents, unable to show love. She shuddered at the thought. All she wanted was someone to love her and one day have a good husband and children of her own. She would love them with all her heart and give them loads of attention. They wouldn't be lacking in anything.

There were some lapses in her memory about her childhood after Gramma Grace went away. What happened to her during those years? Why couldn't she remember her childhood? The memories began when she was in high school. Her thoughts went right to her first boyfriend, Brian. They had dated only for a few months and suddenly he was gone. He never told her that he didn't want to see her anymore. What happened to him?

What was going on? Did her parents do something to frighten Brian away? She did mention to her mother about him. Did her mother share this with her father? Athena didn't trust her father. He never spoke to her unless he had to reprimand her about something she said or did. She never knew what it was like to have a kind and caring father who would listen to her. They never exchanged a kind word to one another. Her mother tried to smooth over things with her by saying, "Your father is tired or doesn't feel well. He has been working too much."

She shook her head and sighed. Thank God for her grandmother.

She thought over what her grandmother had told her about Justin. She didn't remember anything after the time they first met at the writing class and had their first date. She couldn't recall their second date. This was strange. What happened in between?

She looked at her calendar and it had been a month since she and Justin had their first date. She was in the hospital recuperating from the accident but where was he? How come he didn't call her if it was only a dream?

Athena picked up her phone and scrolled through calls received until she came to Justin's. She called and held her breath. Would he answer?

CHAPTER TEN

"Hello? Who is this?"

Athena took a deep breath and answered, "Hi Justin. It's Athena."

"Athena? How are you? Where have you been? I tried to call you."

Athena began to cry. She was too choked up to continue.

Justin waited patiently for her to calm down and asked, "What's wrong, Athena? Please tell me."

She explained about her dream that she thought was real and how she ended up in the hospital for a month. She left out the fact that they may be engaged.

"Are you all right? I don't understand. You were in an accident with me but then I wasn't there? But you still had an accident but no one was in the car with you?"

"Yes. I know it sounds absolutely crazy but that is what I dreamt and then woke up in the hospital. I kept asking for you because I truly believed you were with me. I don't understand it either. I won't blame you if you think that I am out of my mind and not want to see me anymore."

"Not at all, Athena. In fact, I'm coming over there right after work. I'll bring dinner. Any preferences to food?"

Athena was shaking all over when she heard this. "Anything would be fine with me, Justin. Thank you. I'm sorry about…"

"What are you sorry about? You were in an accident and I didn't know about it. I was worried and didn't know who to call to check up on you. I even came by your house but of course you weren't there because you were in the hospital at the time."

"You did? You came by here to see me?"

"Yes, why wouldn't I? When I tried to call you a few times before our date just to talk but you didn't answer your phone. Then I came by for our date and you didn't answer the door. I started to worry that something was wrong."

"My phone was dead so I couldn't get any calls. Thank you for worrying about me, Justin."

"Listen, I have some briefs to finish up and then I will be over after 5:00. We can talk some more at that time."

"Okay. Sounds good to me. It will be so nice to see you again. I've missed you."

"Me too. See you later."

Athena suddenly felt very tired. She laid down on the couch, covered herself with an afghan and was soon fast asleep. She woke up a few hours later and looked at the clock. It was almost 4:00.

She freshened up and waited patiently. It felt like a whole day until Justin arrived with their dinners. When she opened the door, he swept her off her feet and kissed her like the first time. It sent tingles down between her legs and her toes even curled. It was incredible. Boy, did she miss him! He finally put her down, set their dinners out on the island and pulled out two stools for them. He had bought a couple of waters so they had all they needed.

He laid out containers of items from a Pu Pu platter and fried rice. He even placed a napkin on her lap and pulled out plastic utensils.

"It looks delicious, Justin. Thank you. I suddenly feel famished."

"That's good. I love a woman who likes to eat."

Athena nearly choked on her first bite at his retort. Does he love her? Is that what he was trying to say?

"Are you okay, Athena?" he looked at her with concern as he tapped her on the back.

"No, I'm fine, Justin. My food went down too quickly before I could swallow." She coughed a few more times in between explaining.

"Did I say something to upset you?"

"No, of course not, Justin. It's just my ineptitude to swallow. I guess I was eating too fast."

"Take your time. I know it is delicious and hard not to want to gulp down especially if you are really hungry. I do that all the time. I eat too fast."

Athena acknowledged him with a smile and a nod as she continued to take smaller bites and swallow more carefully.

"So, tell me more about the dream you had and what happened when you got to the hospital. Were you seriously injured?"

Athena explained more about the dream, leaving out again the fact that they were possibly engaged and added, "No, I had bumps and bruises, luckily because I landed on a mound of mud next to the stream. The doctor said that saved me from being more severely injured. No broken bones or anything like that, thank goodness. I did bang my head as I was thrown out of the car and that put me out for a while or so they told me. It's hard to know what is real and not part of my dream. I saw myself in the car trapped in my seatbelt but that wasn't what actually happened. I was also so sure that you were there with me and that you may have…." Athena stopped when she became too emotional again. She looked down at her hand – no ring, so there was no engagement. It was all a dream.

"Oh, Athena, I didn't mean to upset you. Are you okay? Thank God you didn't break any bones or suffer more serious injuries. How do you feel now?"

"I'm fine now. I had a little nap before you came. But I still need to see my family doctor and a psychiatrist again soon."

"A psychiatrist?"

"Yes, he wants to make sure that I am doing better with the nightmares that I have from time to time. He said that I may still be in shock over the accident."

"You could be. Oh, I see. Maybe that is a good thing to do – see him again for closure. Do you have nightmares often?"

"Yes, I have always had nightmares since I was in college. I don't remember having them before then though." Athena's face took on a frown as she concentrated trying to remember about her childhood.

"Maybe we shouldn't talk about this now. You are getting too anxious. I don't want you to get yourself sick over worrying about things. You must get rest and take care of yourself. You should lie down and rest some more. I can clean things up here after we finish eating."

"No, Justin. I don't want you to leave yet. We haven't seen each other in so long and I am enjoying talking to you. I'm sorry I do get upset when I try to remember things from my childhood. There are some things I don't like to talk about and one of them is my parents. They are strange."

"Oh, I see. So, you don't want me to meet them?"

"Well…yes. I don't introduce any of my friends male or female to them."

"I don't understand, Athena. Most teens have trouble with their parents but by the time you are in your twenties parents become more acceptable."

"Yeah, maybe yours did. Mine will never be acceptable," Athena sighed and nibbled on a Crab Rangoon.

"I guess I don't understand. Maybe you should tell me a little about them and what makes them strange."

"Do you really want to meet them?"

"Yes, I do. They made you and you are perfect. How bad can they be?" Justin grinned and patted her gently on the arm.

Athena felt speechless at that. She continued to eat and dabbed her mouth with her napkin. She swallowed and cleared her throat, "Well, I better tell you a little about them beforehand. After I explain you may change your mind about meeting them."

Justin listened as she relayed how doting they were on her since her sister's death as a baby; how she never wanted to share things with them and only shared her private thoughts in her diary or at times with her grandmother Grace. She didn't tell him, however, that she did that telepathically.

"Did you ever try to talk to them about things that may have troubled you growing up?"

"No...well, yes, one time I did. It was when I dated a boy in high school, Brian Barker. We had only been dating a short time. I told my mother about him one day and the next day I was supposed to meet Brian after his football practice but he never showed up. In fact he didn't make the practice either. No one knew where he was. It was as if he had dropped off the face of the earth. I never saw him again."

Justin sat looking puzzled and held his head in his hands as he thought over what to say next. "I see. I don't really see but I am as puzzled over what you said as you are. That is strange. You never heard from him again? No one else did either?"

"No, no one ever said anything about where he had gone. Nothing!"

"Oh. There has to be an explanation. His parents maybe took him out of school abruptly and moved away to take a new job or something like that."

"Right, but wouldn't they have given notice to the school and/or teachers. Also, Brian would have wanted to let me know. He was not the type to do something like that – just disappear without a note or explanation. It didn't make sense then and it still doesn't now."

"Yes, I can see that. I'm sorry I don't have any advice for you. Did you love him?"

"No, I barely got to know him. We were too young to know that anyway. But he was a nice guy and always kind and caring and gentle - like you."

"Oh, umm…that's nice. Thank you. My parents taught me always to be kind to everyone. As for being a gentleman, that I got from my father. He is a true gentleman and a loving and caring father. He treats my mother like a queen. I am fortunate to have them both."

Athena smiled as she watched Justin's eyes glaze over with admiration and emotion talking about his parents. He truly was blessed to have them. She only wished her parents were as kind and sensitive.

"You really are blessed to have such wonderful parents. I'm happy for you. You are what they taught you to be."

"Thank you, Athena. I will always treat you like a queen as my father has done with my mother. Now I think my queen has to rest. You just got back from the hospital and have to take it easy. Right? Didn't your doctor give you instructions not to overdo?"

"Yes, he did. I don't think having dinner with my boyfriend is overdoing it. Do you?"

"No, I guess not. Boyfriend? Am I officially your boyfriend?" He smiled broadly.

"I think so. You called me your queen. Maybe I should call you my king instead?" Athena chuckled.

"Well, okay by me. The king has now spoken. I think it's time for me to put away the leftovers for your lunch tomorrow and clean up so you can go lie down or better yet get ready for bed."

Athena raised her eyebrows at him. "Ready for bed?"

"Well, you know what I mean. You get ready for bed and I will take care of all this. Now let me do this for you. Okay? I will call you tomorrow to see how you are feeling."

"Okay, that sounds good to me. Can you please kiss me goodnight so I can have a good night's sleep without any nightmares?"

Athena puckered up and he met her lips in a delightful kiss. She wrapped her arms around his neck and held on tight. She didn't want the kiss to end.

Justin gently took her arms off his shoulders. He kissed her gently one more time then pushed her toward her bedroom so he could do the cleanup and go home.

"Good night, Athena. Sleep well."

"Thank you, Justin, for dinner and for everything. Talk to you tomorrow. Good night." She sashayed away and got ready for bed. She fell asleep so quickly she didn't even hear Justin leave.

CHAPTER ELEVEN

The car was racing around the curve. She was holding on for dear life. She looked over to see who was driving and saw her father. She heard her mother's voice in the back seat. "Slow down, Arnie. Please slow down!"

She turned toward her mother's voice and yelled back, "Why is Dad driving so fast?"

Her mother didn't answer. The car was careening around a sharp curve and not slowing down at all.

She heard a crash and then silence. She was alone on the side of the road and no longer in the car. Where were her parents?

She thrashed in bed and woke herself up. She was covered in sweat and her nightgown was all tangled up around her from all her thrashing.

What did this nightmare mean? Were her parents going to die? Was she? Why did she keep dreaming about a car crash with different people in it?

Athena got out of bed and grabbed her diary to record her dream. She sighed and decided she wasn't going to get much sleep for a while. She went into the kitchen to prepare a cup of green tea to relax her. She noticed how clean her kitchen looked. Justin really did a good job cleaning up. He was definitely a keeper. His mother taught him well.

She sipped her tea and wrote in her diary about yesterdays' lunch with Dr. Jasper and dinner with Justin. There were now two men in her life, so to speak. Did she love one of them? Did she have feelings for the other one?

She thought over what Justin had said about his parents and how much he loved them. She only wished she felt the same about her parents. She really couldn't say there was love there. Was there?

She finished up her tea and her notes and went back to bed. It was only 4:00 a.m. It was too early to stay up. She closed her eyes. The last thoughts in her head were about her parents and her childhood.

*****

"Mommy, I want Gramma Grace. Why can't she come back here? Don't you and Daddy like her?"

"Of course, Athena. We like her. She is…well…"

"What, Mommy? What is she?"

"I think you are too young to understand. One day I will explain when you are older."

Athena slinked off to her room and sulked. She couldn't understand why they didn't want Gramma Grace with them anymore. She missed her and loved her so much. Maybe that was why they didn't want her around. Athena loved her more than she loved her parents.

Her mind raced forward to when she was ten years old. Gramma Grace had been gone for five years now but they still kept in touch telepathically. This Athena did not understand, but was happy to be able to spend time this way with her grandmother.

Her mother was outside her room one day and listening in to her conversation with her grandmother. She passed by and looked in. Athena glanced up from her card game and gave her mother a tight smile.

"What are you doing, Athena? Who are you talking to?"

"No one, Mommy. I was talking to myself and my dolls. We're playing cards."

"Oh, I see. Okay. Have fun. I will be making lunch soon. I'll call you."

"Okay, Mommy." Athena went back to her game and whispered to her grandmother, "I think Mommy heard us talking together."

"Did she? I wouldn't worry about her. Keep an eye out for your father though. Okay, dear? I know he wouldn't like us conversing together like this."

"Why not, Gramma? Doesn't he like you?"

"No, unfortunately he does not get along with me."

"Why not?"

"I guess you are old enough to know that he doesn't like me because I see through him. I don't think he is good enough for my daughter. He is not a kind man. Watch yourself around him. He can be mean. You tell me if he is ever mean to you, Athena. Promise me?"

"Okay, Gramma. I promise you. He doesn't even talk to me or even look at me unless he thinks I did something wrong. Then he gives me an angry look and tells me to go to my room. Mommy seems to be afraid of him. She always looks away when he is angry. I noticed the other day she was sad and crying when I came down for breakfast. She was wiping her eyes and holding her arm as if it hurt her."

"Really? Did you ask her what was wrong?"

"Yes, I did. She said nothing was wrong."

"Well, keep an eye out for her. I fear she is in danger."

"Danger? What kind of danger, Gramma?"

***

Athena raced forward to when she was fourteen and waiting outside the park for her boyfriend, Brian. She waited for half an hour and watched the football players come off the field and go into the locker rooms. She waited until they began to come out. She looked at each face but didn't see Brian. She jumped off the stadium seats and went over to a couple of the players who were coming toward her.

She asked them, "Where is Brian Barker?"

The two boys looked at her and shrugged their shoulders. "Haven't seen him," one boy replied.

"Do you know why he wasn't at practice?"

"No, I don't," the other boy answered.

They walked away and ignored her. She was so upset she rushed home before someone could see the tears threatening to fall. When she arrived home, her mother was sitting at the kitchen table and clearly upset over something.

"What's wrong, Mom?"

"Nothing, dear."

"What happened to your wrist? It's all black and blue! Where's Dad?"

"I fell, honey. He went out. He had something to do."

"Do you need help making supper? Your wrist must be bothering you. You keep rubbing it. Do you want some ice on it?"

"Yes, that would be good. Ice would help too. I have chicken defrosting in the refrigerator and some broccoli. You can make rice like I taught you."

"Okay, Mom. You rest with ice on your wrist and I will take care of dinner."

"Thank you, dear."

Athena busied herself making dinner and set the table. Her mother sat there with the ice on her wrist and didn't move until a car was heard coming into the garage. She then jumped up and ran to the bathroom.

"Where are you going, Mom? Dinner is almost ready."

The door opened and in walked her father. He looked angry. His face was beet red and he was perspiring. He passed by without looking at her but asked gruffly, "Where's your mother?"

Athena was taken back by his angry manner and didn't answer right away. When he turned toward her and reached out to grip her arm she pulled away and answered, "She went to the bathroom."

"Why isn't she making dinner?"

"She hurt her wrist. I told her I would cook to give her a chance to put ice on it."

He disappeared and went looking for his wife.

Athena could hear yelling from them and went closer to make out what they were saying. It sounded like, "What did you do? Why?" from her mother.

From her father she heard, "It had to be done. He wasn't right for her."

Athena hurried back to the stove and stirred the rice as her parents came downstairs and sat at the table.

"Is dinner ready yet, Athena?" her mother asked meekly.

"Yes, almost ready. I will take the chicken out of the oven now. The rice is done and so is the broccoli. I'll bring it all over, Mom. You don't have to help."

Dinner was served in silence. No one wanted to talk. Her mother was still nursing her wrist which could be broken while her father gulped down his food, pushed away from the table and stomped out of the room without a word. A few minutes later the front door slammed.

Athena had lost her appetite but managed to eat a little and helped her mother clean up. She suggested, "Mom, I think you have to go to the hospital and have an x-ray. You may have broken your wrist. Do you want me to call Dr. Nettles?"

"Yes, that would be better, dear. Please call Dr. Nettles. He will know what to do."

Athena made the call and Dr. Nettles came right over. When he arrived Athena escorted him to the living room where her mother was sitting with her wrist elevated and packed with ice.

"What happened, Carla?"

"I fell when I went to pick up dirty clothes and carry it to the laundry room. I was just clumsy."

Dr. Nettles exchanged looks with Athena and she shrugged her shoulders and shook her head. "I wasn't here when it happened, so I don't know anything."

"Okay, Athena. No worries. Let me check it out and see if it is broken. If it is, Carla, I will take you to the emergency room and set it. Where is your husband, Carla?"

"I don't know. He went out." She didn't meet Dr. Nettles' eyes when she said this.

"Did he know I was coming over?"

"No, I didn't tell him."

Athena again shrugged her shoulders and raised her eyebrows at the doctor.

"Well, it looks like it is broken, Carla. Let's get you over to the hospital and taken care of. I'll get a prescription to give you for the pain later so you can sleep. It will give you some discomfort, dear. But don't worry, I'll take care of everything."

"Thank you, Doctor. I don't know what I would have done without you." Carla sniffled as she cradled her wrist.

"It's okay, Mom. Dr. Nettles will take care of you. I will stay here and clean up the kitchen. When you get back I will help you get to bed. Okay?"

"Thank you, Athena. You are a good girl."

Dr. Nettles whispered to Athena, "Be careful, young lady. Call me if you need anything when your father gets back. Okay?"

Athena looked at the doctor and scrunched up her face, "Do you think my father did that to my mother?"

"I'm not saying anything of the sort. I am only telling you to be careful. Stay out of his way. He tends to be angry about things that don't go his way. He won't like that I took your mother to the hospital. If he gives you a hard time, tell him to come to the hospital and talk to me there."

Athena sighed and said, "Okay. I'll be careful and also tell him to see you if he has any questions."

"Thanks, Athena. Go to your room after you clean up and lock your door. Just do that for me. Okay?"

She nodded and returned to the kitchen to clean up as quickly as she could before her father returned.

She was clearly nervous and wondering about what the doctor had said about her father and his temper.

She managed to get to her room in the nick of time before her father came storming into the house slamming doors as he searched for her and her mother.

"Carla, Athena, where are you?"

Athena pushed her bureau in front of the door just in case he tried to get in. He sounded extremely angry. She had never heard him like this. As he came closer to her door he yelled, "Athena, are you in there? Where in the hell is your mother?"

He tried the door and rattled the knob. "Why did you lock your door? Where is your mother? Answer me now? Do you hear me?"

"Yes…Yes…I…I hear you, Dad. She went to the hospital with Dr. Nettles to set her wrist. It was broken."

"What? Dr. Nettles came here? What's wrong with her?" He ran down the stairs and out the front door slamming it and nearly breaking it in two.

***

Athena thrashed in bed as she relived memories that had somehow been buried. The dreams continued.

Later that evening Dr. Nettles brought her mother back home. Her father was right behind them in his car. He had just missed a chance to bring Carla home.

When they arrived Athena came rushing out to meet her mother and help her into the house. Dr. Nettles handed Athena her mother's prescription and turned to get back in his car but was stopped by Arnold Stone.

He wore an angry expression and his face was as red as a lobster that just came out of the pot – hot and steaming.

"What do you think you are doing, Dr. Nettles?" He screamed in the doctor's face.

"Hello, Mr. Stone. I brought your wife to the hospital to set her wrist which was broken, and now I brought her home."

"Who told you to come here and put your nose into our business?" The lobster continued to steam and sweat.

"Listen, I came because your wife needed help. Evidently you were not around to supply that assistance."

"I…I was coming right back to take her to the hospital."

"Really? This is hours later. When did you think you were going to take her, after she was in a great deal of pain?" Dr. Nettles met Arnold Stone's angry stare with one of his own.

"Never mind. Get out of here now. We don't need you anymore."

"I plan to leave, Mr. Stone. But I will be calling back after my rounds to check on Carla. I would suggest that you let her rest and recuperate if you know what is good for you."

"What? What did you say?"

"You heard me, Mr. Stone. I can report your abuse. I have documentation – photos of her wrist, arm and back showing the bruises."

"She…she's just clumsy, that's all. I didn't do anything to her," he stammered and turned away from the doctor to go into the house.

"Remember what I said about reporting you, Arnold. I am serious. Stay away from Carla and Athena!"

Arnold stormed into the house slamming the door as was now usual for him.

He marched up the stairs to see his wife and give her a piece of his mind.

Athena was in the room with her mother making her comfortable in bed. She looked with alarm at her father standing in the doorway watching them. He came forward with his fists raised.

She cried out, "No Daddy, don't do it! Leave Mommy alone. She is hurt and needs to rest."

Carla shirked away from him and buried her face in the pillows.

Arnold stopped short of hitting his wife as Athena stepped in front of her mother to prevent him from hurting her anymore.

"No, Daddy, I won't let you hurt her again. I'll call the police. Leave here now or I will call them."

Her father put his fists down and left the room. He went down to the kitchen and rummaged around looking for something to drink. He banged cabinet doors and pots and pans around making as much noise as he possibly could to disturb and punish his wife for calling her doctor.

Carla looked at her daughter who was in tears. "Athena, sweetheart, sit here." She patted the side of her bed.

"Why is he like this, Mom? Doesn't he like Dr. Nettles?"

"He is jealous, that's all. He wants all my attention and doesn't want me to have any help from another man."

"Well, he didn't offer to take you to the hospital. What else were you going to do?"

"I know, Athena. Relax now. Don't worry. He won't bother us anymore tonight. He will drink himself into a stupor and fall asleep. I suggest you go to your room and lock yourself in. Lock my door too when you leave. I don't want him in here with me until he is sober." She swiped her hand across Athena's brow and handed her a key to lock the door.

"Okay, Mom. Are you all right now? You need to take this medicine for pain that Dr. Nettles handed to me. Do you need anything else?"

"No, dear. I'm fine. Thank you. Can you put my glass of water back on the nightstand?"

"Sure. I hope you will be able to sleep now that you took that pain medication."

"I'll be fine, Athena. Now go to your room and stay safe. Okay? I love you. Thank you for helping me today."

Athena went to her room and felt a warm feeling on her brow from where her mother had touched her. It was tingling in an odd way and suddenly she felt very tired. She changed into her nightgown and locked her door and went to bed. She wondered why she had locked her door but sighed heavily and closed her eyes.

CHAPTER TWELVE

Athena woke up later than usual after her night of the horrific memories that had been long hidden. She wondered how she had forgotten all about her father's abusive nature toward her mother.

She had to talk to her mother and find out if her father was still abusing her. Why had she been hiding this? Why didn't Athena remember until now?

Athena sat with a cup of coffee in front of her and some scrambled eggs and toast. She was surprisingly hungry after her long night of trauma. She ate quickly and cleaned up.

A lot of things were not making sense to her. First of all, why was she having these dreams? What did her mother do to her that day when she touched her forehead? Did she wipe away her memories somehow? Was her mother a witch or something like her grandmother – a clairvoyant? Did she have some of these powers herself?

There were too many questions that had to be answered. She was worried about her mother more than ever now. Would her father somehow kill her mother during his angry outbursts? She was feeling sorry for her mother. She felt guilty for not being patient with her when she called to ask how she was doing. She would somehow make it up to her.

The more she thought about her father and his explosive personality she wondered about other things. What about her boyfriend, Brian? Did he hurt him in some way? She remembered overhearing their conversation of someone not being good enough for her. Did they mean Brian?

Her mind flooded with possibilities and she cried out in alarm. What about Justin? Would he go after Justin if he found out they were dating? Would he be crazy enough to hurt him?

Athena had to call Justin to make sure he was okay. She went back into the bedroom to pick up her cell off the nightstand where it was charging.

She scrolled through her calls until she saw Justin's number from when he last called her and went back to the kitchen to sit at the island.

Athena waited for his phone to ring. She nervously tapped her nails on the island and counted the rings, one, two, three, four, and then his voicemail came on. She hung up before she could leave a cryptic message that he wouldn't understand.

He would surely think she was crazy if she told him about her dreams and how worried she was about his safety.

She sighed and left her phone on the kitchen island and went to take a shower. Maybe under the warm water she would feel better and make sense of what she had seen in her dreams.

While she was in the shower she thought she heard a ringing. She grabbed a towel and wrapped it around her and carefully got out of the shower to get her phone.

By the time she got to the kitchen the ringing had stopped. She looked at the phone to see if someone had left a message. It must have been Justin.

There were no messages. She went back to dry off and get dressed while pondering who could have called since she didn't recognize the number.

It could have been her mother again asking her if she was okay. But it wasn't her number. She had to laugh about that but not in a good way. It should be her asking her mother how she was.

She had to ask her mother about her safety too. Maybe she was somehow trying to tell Athena that she was in danger. She was always in a hurry to get off the phone with her mother thinking that she was just being possessive. Maybe all she wanted was to talk to her daughter and feel safe for a little while. She must be so lonely living with a man who couldn't control his temper. What kind of life was that for her mother? She couldn't even talk to her husband about everyday things. He would jump to conclusions about things that weren't true, especially about Dr. Nettles. Did he think that her mother was in love with Dr. Nettles? Is that why he was so angry that day when Dr. Nettles came to their house and took care of her mother?

She thought over the years about how many times Dr. Nettles came over to their house when her father was not home. She couldn't count how many. There were several that she knew of. He could have come over when she was in school too.

She wondered about that. They were quite compatible, easily talked and laughed a lot together. She remembered one time she came home earlier from school when her after school projects were cancelled. Dr. Nettles was sitting on the couch with her mother and they were laughing about something. They appeared to be completed taken with each other. She had noticed that her mother's eyes were sparkling like she had never seen before. She looked happy too. She was usually morose and quiet.

Athena had tiptoed up the stairs to her room so as not to disturb them. She was busy with her homework and didn't realize the doctor was still there until she heard his voice across the hall from her room. She peeked out from her door and saw him kiss her mother on the cheek and give her a big hug before he went downstairs.

Athena didn't give it much thought at the time. But now when she thought it over, she realized that it may have been more than just a friendship between them. She felt happy one moment for her mother to have found someone who cared for her. But on the other hand, she was frightened for the possibility that her father would find out about their close relationship and do harm to the doctor.

She loved Dr. Nettles like a father because she had no relationship with her own father. She couldn't get close to him. He didn't allow anyone to get to know him or feel comfortable around him.

Dr. Nettles was always there for her. Whenever she felt upset about something, she called him. He was the one to make her feel better. She never even thought about going to her father. She had talked to her mother over the years but she always appeared to be somewhere else. She didn't focus when Athena would ask her something. She now understood why she was not really there. Her mind was somewhere else. She lived in fear of her husband and probably for her daughter's safety too.

Athena remembered one particular day that she came home from school and her father was home early. When she walked into the house she heard screaming from her mother and her father yelling and things being knocked down.

She hurried upstairs to see what was going on. She had called out to her mother, "Mom, are you all right?" She waited but no response. The next second her father stormed out of her parent's room and pushed her aside to go downstairs.

She waited until he was gone before opening her parent's bedroom door. Her mother was lying on the bed and crying.

"Mom, are you okay?"

"Oh, Athena, I didn't know you were home. I'm fine, dear. I'm just a little tired and need to rest. Do you want to order a pizza for dinner? I'm not really that hungry."

"Umm, sure, Mom. I'll order one and save you and Dad a couple of pieces."

"Don't worry about your father. He won't be coming back for a while."

"Where did he go, Mom? Is he angry about something?"

"He is always angry about something, honey. Don't worry about it. He probably went to the local bar. Go do your homework and then you can order pizza at 5:00. Okay? I'm going to sleep for a little while."

"Okay, Mom. If you need anything, let me know. Okay? I love you."

"Love you too, honey."

Athena went back to her room to finish up her homework and at 5:00 she ordered her pizza. Her father never came home that night.

She thought it was funny that she was remembering all these things now. Why was that? Did her mother finally take off the spell or whatever that kept her from remembering these things?

She came out of her musings when the phone rang. She grabbed it and looked at the call coming in. It was Justin.

"Justin? How are you? I tried to call you before but I didn't leave a message."

"Yes, I saw your number come up but I was in a meeting with my colleagues about a new case we are working on. Sorry I didn't get back to you. I couldn't pick it up at that time and the meeting went on and on. Oh, sorry. I'm going on and on. What's wrong, Athena? Your voice sounds funny."

"Oh, umm, nothing is wrong, Justin. I needed to hear your voice."

"Are you sure, Athena? You know that you can tell me anything. I will not judge you. Are you having nightmares again?"

"Well, kind of strange dreams about my childhood."

"Oh, what kind of dreams? Did you do some funny things when you were a kid?" Justin chuckled.

"Not really but it was stuff that I had somehow locked away in my mind and had forgotten."

"That does sound ominous, Athena. Do you want to share them with me? I can come by tonight and we can talk about them. I will bring dinner."

"Okay, that sounds good. Thank you. I think I should tell you some of these things. I hope you won't think I am crazy though."

"I would never think you were crazy, Athena. Come on, I think you know that I am a good listener and don't judge others harshly."

"I guess so. Okay. Well, I don't want to keep you. You're at work. Sorry for bothering you."

"You are never a bother, my dear. It is always wonderful to hear your voice. I miss you when I don't see you or talk to you. We need to do something about that, don't we?"

"What?"

"You are funny, Athena. I am trying to say that we need to see each other more than just once a week and we should be talking daily to one another. What do you think about that?"

"Well, I guess so. I mean…I miss seeing you more often too. We are going out on Saturday though. That's not too far away and we are talking now."

"Yes, we are and I will be over closer to 6:00 tonight with dinner. I will surprise you with something. Okay?"

"Okay. I like surprises. Thank you."

"You don't have to thank me yet. I hope you will like my surprise."

"I'm sure I will, Justin."

"See you then, my lovely Athena."

"Bye, Justin."

Athena felt her a blush come to her cheeks when he said this. She really believed she could tell him anything and he would accept her and understand. He was sweet and kind. She really lucked out finding him. She only hoped she could keep this luck going and no harm would come to him. She had to keep him private from her parents. She wasn't ready to share him with them for fear of what could happen.

***

At 5:30 Athena finished putting on her makeup and a different outfit so she could look nice for Justin. She was excited to see him again and wondered what he was going to bring for dinner and a surprise.

She paced the living room until the doorbell sounded. She glanced in the mirror in the foyer for a quick look before answering the door.

Justin stood with a large bag in one hand while the other hand was hidden behind his back. He was looking good enough to kiss, which was what she wanted to do right away.

She ushered Justin in, put her arms around his neck and pulled him down to her height for a kiss. He responded in kind and put the food bag down on a nearby table and squeezed her until she thought she wouldn't be able to breathe.

"I'm sorry, Athena. Did I squeeze you a little too much? When you are in my arms I don't want to ever let go. Did I tell you how beautiful you look tonight?"

"Umm, no. But, thank you," Athena blushed as she backed into the kitchen not taking her eyes off of him.

Justin picked up the food, placed the bag on the kitchen island and brought out his other hand with a surprise.

Athena's eyes opened wide as he presented her with a gorgeous bouquet of every flower you could imagine which produced a riot of colors. Her breath caught in her throat and she found she couldn't speak.

"Are you okay, Athena?" Justin's furrowed brow showed his concern.

"Yes, I'm fine, Justin. I never expected so many flowers and such a beautiful combination of colors. They are incredible! Thank you so much. I'll get a large vase and put them in some water. They are too gorgeous to let wilt."

"Did I surprise you? I like doing that."

"Yes, you definitely did. Thank you so much. I love all kinds of flowers. I'll enjoy these for many days ahead."

"I didn't know what kind of flowers you like, so I got a few of all the flowers in the shop. The person who waited on me must have thought I was crazy but he didn't say. I think he was happy to sell so many flowers at one time."

"I can see how he would be. This is an amazing bouquet. I've never seen one like it. In fact, no one ever gave me flowers before."

"Really? You never received flowers from other suitors? I can't believe that. You are so beautiful. How could those guys be so stupid not to give you something to highlight your beauty?"

"Well, it wasn't guys, only one guy I dated more than once. He never gave me flowers and probably didn't realize how much I love them."

"I'm happy to know that I am the first guy you dated who gave you a bouquet that is worthy of your beauty."

"Wow, Justin. You say the most unexpected things. You surprise me with your complimentary skills."

"Why, thank you, my dear. I guess I took lessons from my father. He gave my mother bouquets of flowers every other day. She loved all kinds of flowers. I would watch her eyes light up when he gave her some and also when her garden produced the first roses. She was so happy, she danced around the house."

"Your parents sound special and loving toward one another. I wish my parents were …," Athena choked up and couldn't go on.

"What's wrong, my sweet? Don't your parents love one another?"

"No, but I don't want to talk about them. Let's see what you brought for dinner. I'm starved." She moved toward the island and pulled out food containers so he wouldn't see the tears threatening to fall.

Justin pitched in, grabbed some plates and utensils and moved the food to them. He had brought Chicken Marsala with pasta and salads and a bottle of wine which he opened right away.

Athena pulled out wine glasses and poured a generous amount for both of them. She took a long sip and sighed.

"Are you okay, Athena?" Justin clinked his glass against hers and took a long sip too. The next minute he looked over at Athena, she was smiling.

"Ah, yes. I feel better now. Thank you, Justin. The Chicken Marsala is delicious," she said between bites and sighs of delight.

"I'm so relieved. I wasn't sure you liked it."

"Justin, never worry about me and food. I like everything and eat like a lumberjack," she chuckled, suddenly feeling relaxed and happy.

"Phew. That's good to know. But, come to think of it, you always eat everything in your plate before I do. Where do you put it all in that little body? You don't have an ounce of fat on you."

"I...I guess I'm lucky. I have always been fortunate not to gain weight even if I don't watch my calories. Thank goodness for that. I do walk a lot and exercise so I can eat even more than normal," she laughed as her eyes sparkled.

"Well, I guess I can share some of mine with you if you need more," Justin chuckled and leaned in to plant a kiss on her nose.

"No need for that. I have some ice cream in the freezer that I plan to bring out for dessert. In fact, I have four different kinds in there."

"Hmm, what kinds?"

"Let me see." She peeked in the freezer and pulled out one at a time. "Chocolate almond, pistachio, sherbet – orange, lime and lemon, and vanilla."

"I like them all. How about you give me a scoop of each? We can share it." Justin grabbed two spoons as Athena scooped out the ice cream and sherbet in a deep dish.

They sat there oohing and aahing as they spooned ice cream into each other's mouths.

"How about some coffee, Justin?"

"Sounds good. I think I need something to push everything else down. I am so full!"

"Me too! It was all delicious. Thank you so much for dinner, Justin."

"My pleasure, my lady." He bowed to her and kissed her hand as she walked by to start the coffee.

He kept his eyes on her and watched her walk away. Athena could feel his eyes on her and smiled. She turned and placed their coffee cups in front of them and leaned over to kiss his tempting lips. She could taste some of the ice cream still there. It was the best tasting kiss she had ever had.

"If I wasn't so full I would carry you to your room and…" He winked at her and smiled.

"Well, if I wasn't so full I would let you," she retorted with a giggle.

They sipped coffees and Athena told Justin about her dreams of her father and his abuse toward her mother. She watched his face as it paled and his brows tightened together.

She sat back and sighed, relieved to get that off her chest with him.

"I'm so sorry, Athena. I didn't realize that. Did he ever hurt you too?"

"No. He didn't, thank goodness. But I think my mother took all his abuse and kept me safe from harm. I didn't realize that all these years. I had kept it all hidden away in my subconscious, I guess."

"Maybe you did because it was too horrific to face. Is your mother doing okay?"

"Yes, I think so. But I do worry every minute now that I remember it all. I will keep checking up on her regularly though."

"That's the thing to do, Athena. Be close to her and watch over her like she did you." Justin pulled her in close for a hug. He didn't want her to see the tears in his eyes for her and her mother.

Athena nestled closer to Justin and sighed. Her heart was heavy. He helped to lighten her load by just being there and listening to her.

What would she ever do without him?

CHAPTER THIRTEEN

The next day Athena still had a warm feeling in the pit of her stomach thinking over the dinner last night with Justin. The food was delicious but more so because he was there to share it with her.

She felt so fortunate to have won his heart. He certainly had captured hers. Who wouldn't love a man like this who did everything to please her?

Over coffee she thought about the dreams she had the previous night involving her mother and father. She had to confront her mother about these dreams and why she was suddenly reliving them.

She poured herself a second cup of strong coffee. She would need it before she called her mother.

She called and waited. Several rings later and there was still no answer from her mother or father. Maybe they were out. Why didn't it go to voicemail?

She took a deep breath and sighed but not in a good way. She feared that something was wrong. Her mother could be in danger. What if her father attacked her mother again? This time he could kill her.

Athena sat near the phone in case her mother called. Maybe she was shopping. She tried to think positively because the alternative was not pleasant.

She called again. This time the phone only rang twice before her mother picked it up.

"Mom? It's Athena. Are you all right?"

"Yes, dear. I'm fine. Why? Is something wrong?"

"Umm, no, but I called you an hour ago and there was no answer. It didn't even go to your voicemail."

"Really? That's strange. I was home cleaning out the refrigerator and freezer. I didn't hear the phone ring."

Athena waited a minute because she could hear her mother banging around the phone.

"What are you doing, Mom?"

"I just checked the voicemail button. It was turned off and the sound was lowered. I didn't do that. I wonder what happened. I luckily noticed your number come up on my phone or I would have missed your call again."

"Mom, is Dad home?"

"No, Athena. He went out a little while ago. I don't expect him home for the rest of the day. He went to visit a friend over in the next city."

"A friend? I didn't know he even had a friend."

"Well, come to think of it, he never mentioned anyone to me either. You know how quiet your father is. He never shares anything with me. Sometimes I wonder why I even …," she choked up and stopped short of saying anymore.

"What, Mom? Are you sorry you married Dad?"

"Never mind, Athena. I don't know what I am saying. Please ignore me. Sometimes I talk too much and say things that I shouldn't."

"No, I don't think you do, Mom. You are always careful what you say especially when Dad is around."

"Oh, right. I sometimes have to be. So, what is going on with you, Athena? Why did you call?"

"Mom, we need to talk. Can you come over here? I don't want to go there in case Dad comes back. We can have lunch together here. I can fix something or we can order in. Whatever you choose."

"Oh, you mean a girls' lunch together? That would be fun! We've never done anything like that before. What's going on, Athena? Are you okay? You are worrying me, dear."

"No, nothing is wrong with me, Mom. I'm fine. There are some things I would like to discuss with you, that's all."

"Do you have a boyfriend that you want to tell me about? Are you engaged?"

"No, Mom, nothing like that to share. Why don't you finish up what you are doing and then come over about noon, okay?"

"Okay, dear. That sounds good. I can't wait. I'll finish up here and be over before noon. Okay?"

"Sure, Mom. Sounds good. Looking forward to seeing you too."

Athena put her phone down and looked around at her house. There were some things to do to clean up and make it look fresh before her mother arrived. She knew her mother would notice anything out of place or an inch of dust if she didn't clear it away.

She sighed and started with the kitchen. Next she pulled out her vacuum and duster and worked on the living room and her bedroom. Her mother wouldn't be going in there but she would use the bathroom across the hall from her bedroom. What was going to stop her mother from peeking into her room to check it out?

Her mother was meticulous with her cleaning and always was because of her father. He was picky about everything. If he found dust and dirt, he would go ballistic if everything wasn't perfect.

Athena thought about this fact and realized that she was just noticing this now about her parents. Their house was always picked up and clean as if no one lived there. She got used to that fact but did notice her friends' houses weren't as neat when she went to visit them.

She knew she was always cleaning her own place because she didn't want her mother to drop in and see it in disarray. She was only one person and thankfully didn't mess things up too much.

She took out the trash from the dinner the night before and sprayed the kitchen with a freshener to get out the smell of the Marsala they had eaten.

She didn't mind the smell. It brought back a sweet memory of when Justin had kissed her good night. She hadn't wanted that kiss to end.

Athena sighed and pushed on with her cleaning. Next she tackled the floors in the kitchen and bathroom. She finally put away all her cleaning products and surveyed the area. She smiled in satisfaction and looked into her refrigerator to find something to make for lunch with her mother. It looked pretty bare so she pulled out her list of restaurants for takeout and decided on the new salad and wrap place. She knew her mother always ate healthy and wouldn't want anything like burgers and fries which Athena was now craving.

She called and ordered a couple of lobster salad wraps and small side salads. Her mother loved lobster. She would definitely be in a good mood to answer her questions after eating.

She picked up the vase of flowers and moved it to her bedroom. If her mother saw it she would have to explain who gave it to her.

A half hour later her mother arrived with a bunch of flowers she had picked up from her garden. She thrust them forward into Athena's hands and kissed her cheek.

"Hi Mom. Thank you. These are beautiful!"

"You're welcome, Athena. Yes, my flowers have been prolific. I love gardening. It keeps me outside and lets me get some fresh air."

"That's good for you, Mom. I haven't done anything with gardens here. I don't own this place so I can't plant anything unless I have an inside garden. That's too much trouble."

"Oh, don't worry about it, dear. You could have an herb garden on your kitchen window, such as some parsley, basil and oregano or some other combinations depending upon what you like to cook."

"Yes, I guess I could. But, I don't cook much with just me. I do a lot of takeout. There are so many places around here that deliver. Speaking of delivery, I ordered something that I know you are going to love from a new wrap place."

"Really? What place is that?"

"Umm, it's called Wrap City. I order wraps and salads from there at least once or twice a week."

"That's good to know that you aren't serving me your favorite - a burger and fries," her mother chuckled.

"No, Mom. I wouldn't do that. I know what you like and don't like to eat. I know I don't always eat right. But I try to eat healthy at least a couple of times a week."

"That's nice, dear." Her mother walked around the kitchen and living room taking everything in. "Your place looks so pristine, honey."

Athena gulped in air in surprise, "Umm, thanks, Mom. I try to keep it neat like you do. I guess I learned how to be a good housekeeper from you."

Before any further discussion about her apartment took place, the doorbell rang.

"That's our lunch, Mom." Athena rushed over to the door and handed the delivery boy a tip and thanked him.

She put plates down and transferred the wraps there, grabbed some napkins, utensils, and poured some iced tea for them announcing, "It's lunch, Mom."

Her mother sat down at the island and smiled. "My favorite, honey. Thank you so much."

"Your welcome, Mom. What kind of dressing do you want? I have a few different kinds."

"Just oil and vinegar would be fine, honey."

"Did you like your lunch, Mom?" Athena watched her mother's face as she dabbed her lips one last time and pushed away from the island.

"It was delicious! I will have to order some time for your father and me. I think he will actually like these wraps with meat and cheese instead of lobster. That would be nice not to have to cook a big meal every night," she sighed.

"You should do that more often. You need a break every week from cooking."

"I agree, Athena. Now I just have to convince your father. That is not an easy thing to do."

Athena didn't respond to this statement but thought it was an opening for her to ask her mother some important questions.

"Mom, I have to ask you some questions. I don't want you to get angry though. These are important to me. I need to know about you and Dad."

"What about me and Dad?" Her face took on a serious expression as she turned to Athena.

Athena felt her heart beating faster as she met the fierce look in her mother's eyes. She straightened up and took a deep breath and began, "Mom, I've been having dreams about you and Dad. They are not pleasant dreams though."

"What are you trying to say, Athena?"

"Well, I dreamt that Dad abused you in the past. I'm worried about what he may do to you now that I am not there with you."

Carla Stone suddenly looked older than her years when she met her daughter's eyes. "Honey, I'm sorry about that. I tried to keep these things from you. I had hoped you wouldn't remember any of them. Your grandmother told me what to do to keep you from harm. I did what I could but maybe not enough."

"What do you mean, Mom? Keep me from harm?"

"Listen, Athena. I know you understand what your grandmother is and what I am also. Now you have the same talents as we do. We can all see into the future and can help others by warning them. We can also make a person forget things by touching them on their foreheads as I did to you when you were young. I didn't want you to remember these things."

"But Mom, I remember them now. Why didn't you stop Dad from hurting you? You should have gotten away from him a long time ago. Do you even love him?"

"Those are difficult things to answer, dear. I wanted to leave many times but I knew that he would find me and hurt you if I did. I didn't want that to happen. You are too precious to me. When I lost your sister, I thought I would die. Then I had you and felt reborn. I thought I could handle anything he did to me as long as he didn't harm you. As to the second question, do I love him? I guess I haven't loved him in a long time. Abuse does that to a person – erases all the love that one felt at one time. I couldn't get it back and gave up with love. As long as I had you, I felt loved and loved you back with all my heart."

"Oh, Mom, I'm so sorry! I love you with all my heart too. I wish I had known sooner about what you have been through. I haven't always been patient with you. Can you forgive me?"

"Oh, Athena, sweetheart. I know you didn't remember until recently because you have been different. I noticed a change in your attitude toward me and your father. Can you understand why I didn't want you to live like that, in fear of your life, as I have had to do?"

"Of course I do, Mom. But why should you continue to do this when I am no longer there for you to worry about. It's time for you to leave. Divorce him now, Mom. You can't stay any longer. He may hurt you more or even kill you one day. Do you want that?"

"No, Athena. But I am in the process of doing that now. I filed for divorce last week. I haven't told him yet but will have to soon. He will receive the divorce papers when he returns home."

"Mom, why don't you stay here? You can sleep in my bed. I'll take the pullout couch. I don't want you to go back home. When Dad receives the papers he will become violent. You can't go back. Let me take you home now so you can pick up some things before he returns. You can stay here as long as you need to."

"Thank you, honey. Okay, that may be a good idea. Let's go now before he returns so I can pack a suitcase."

Athena picked up her keys and cell and followed her mother out to her car.

"We can go in my car, honey." Looking at the car in the garage when Athena opened it, Carla asked, "Is this your new car since you totaled the other one?"

"Yes Mom, unfortunately it couldn't be fixed. This one is from the insurance money just to get me around. I'll probably buy a better one after I get myself a job. I was planning on having you put your car in my garage so Dad wouldn't see it."

"All right. That sounds good. He will come looking for me here first."

"Don't worry. I will alert the police if I see him. They have to know what abuse you have had at his hands. "

Athena pulled her car out of the garage and put her mother's there instead and closed the door. She opened her car door for her mother and they drove away.

Her mother continued to explain, "My lawyer told me to file for a restraining order on him. I did that already too. He won't be able to come near me."

"Good thinking, Mom. I will feel better knowing that he can't touch you again. We're here. Let me help you pack some things. Take as much as you can because you may not be able to come back."

Athena pulled out two suitcases from the top of her mother's closet, folded and placed several outfits inside. Her mother packed her cosmetics in a case and picked out underwear, pants, tops and shoes.

"Are you all done, Mom? Do you need more help?"

"No, dear. I think I have everything I will need for a month or more. I can wash clothes at your house anyway. I'm having a difficult time choosing what

I want to bring. I hate to leave anything behind. It may be gone when I try to come back."

"Why? Do you think Dad will throw away your stuff? If that's the case then I will pack more of your stuff. Let's take as much as we can. Only leave stuff you really don't care too much about."

"Okay, let's do that. Good idea. I may never come back here again."

"Well, the house is still half yours, Mom. Dad will have to make a decision to sell his half to you or you both sell it outright. That might be the best way to go."

"Yes, I think so too," Carla said sadly.

"Oh, Mom. It's going to be all right. You can stay with me indefinitely. Okay?"

"Thank you, Athena. I appreciate what you are doing for me. I don't deserve it though. I haven't always been the best mother to you. For that, I am sorry."

"Mom, I have no complaints. You are a good mother and always have been. I didn't realize, or I should say, didn't remember the terrible things you were going through. For that, I am sorry."

"You don't have to be sorry about anything, Athena. You are the joy in my life and the reason I go on."

Mother and daughter hugged with tears in their eyes, finished their packing and loaded up the car. They never looked back as they drove away from the only home they both had known.

Time would tell what was going to happen when Athena's father arrived back there.

CHAPTER FOURTEEN

A few days later in the early hours of the morning there was a loud banging at Athena's front door. Athena drew the drapes aside at her front window and peeked out. Her father stood there with his fist raised to bang again. His face was beet red and his forehead dripped of perspiration.

Athena raced back to her bedroom where her mother was sitting up and shaking all over.

"It's okay, Mom. I'm calling the police. He can't come in and hurt you."

"Hello, my name is Athena Stone. I want to report a disturbance from an unwanted visitor at my front door. My father is trying to come in. My mother has filed a restraining order against him. He has abused her in the past many times."

"I see. What is your mother's name?"

"Carla Stone, and my father is Arnold Stone."

Athena answered more questions and gave the officer her address and her parents' address too. He promised to send out a couple of officers directly.

She sighed in relief and related to her mother what the officer said. They were both up now with the incessant banging at the door.

Her father was not going away. He began yelling, "I know you are in there, Carla. Open up now! Do you hear me?"

Athena hugged her mother and guided her to the kitchen to make a cup of tea to calm her down until the police arrived.

After they had finished their second cup of tea the police arrived with lights flashing. They watched from the front window as the police escorted her father to the cruiser in handcuffs.

One officer knocked at the door waiting to speak with Athena and her mother.

"Thank you, officer, for coming so quickly," Athena announced as she watched her father now sitting in the cruiser and yelling out to her. At least she couldn't hear him anymore.

She couldn't make out what he was saying but surmised that he was quite angry at both of them.

"Are you Athena Stone?" the officer queried as he glanced at her mother standing next to her.

"Yes, I am. This is my mother who has filed a restraining order against my father."

"Sorry, ladies, that this had to happen to you. I have the restraining order in hand and have read and explained it to your father and your husband. We will take him back to the station and have a little talk with him and his lawyer. You need not worry about him for now. If he does try to come back, you must call us. We will pick him up again. That is all we can do."

"Okay, thank you, officer," Athena and her mother announced in unison.

They closed the door and watched the police drive away.

"What am I going to do if he comcs back again? What if he comes here when you are not here?"

"Mom, please don't think about that now. I haven't started working yet and if I go out you will go with me. Okay?'

"No, I can't be trailing along with you like a puppy dog, Athena. This is not fair to you. I think I need to find a place of my own. That way he won't know where I am."

"Mom, he will keep coming back here looking for you no matter what. I think you are safe here. The police will come back and get him again if necessary."

They talked for a few hours after breakfast and felt better about Carla's future without her husband. Before they could continue their conversation the phone rang. Athena looked at her cell and noticed an unfamiliar number.

"Who is it, dear?"

"I don't know, Mom. I better answer it."

"Hello? Who is this?"

"Athena, sweetheart, it's Gramma Grace. I just flew in and am at the airport getting my luggage. Can you come pick me up?"

"Gramma Grace? I didn't know you were coming in today. You said you would be calling to let me know when you were coming."

"Well, that's what I'm doing now. I'm here," she chuckled but stopped when she picked up something in her granddaughter's tone.

"What's wrong, Athena?"

"Umm, well, I…"

Her mother stepped closer and pulled the phone away from Athena. "Let me talk to her, honey."

"Mother, why are you here?"

"Carla? What are you doing at Athena's? Is everything all right, dear?"

"Not really, Mother. There have been some new developments. I guess it is time to tell you. But, of course, you probably already know."

"You finally left Arnold, dear?"

"Yes, Mother, I did!" Carla snapped back.

"Well, it is long overdue, dear." Her voice softened and she asked, "Are you okay?"

Carla changed her sharp tone in response, "Yes, I'm fine. He came here to get me but the police took him away. I had filed a restraining order against him."

"Good girl! Well, why don't you both come and get me. I'll take you out for dinner later tonight. I have my luggage now and am waiting out front."

Carla told Athena what her mother had said and handed the phone back to her daughter.

"Gramma Grace, we're leaving now. Be there in half an hour. Okay?"

Once the three generations were settled back at Athena's now small overcrowded apartment, they sat down for some tea. They would need more tea as they continued to discuss the years that Carla had wasted staying with Arnold, according to Gramma Grace.

Gramma Grace explained why she had left her daughter's house many years before, hoping to give closure for her daughter and granddaughter.

"I never got along with Arnold. We didn't like each other from the beginning. He didn't want me there. After you were born, Athena, I waited a little longer so that you would at least remember me. I also wanted to teach you a little about connections so we could stay somewhat close even if I wasn't near you."

"I figured as much, Mother. I knew you were up to something. Each time I walked by Athena's room I could hear her talking. I knew she was talking to you."

"You did? You knew? Why didn't you ever tell me that, Mom?"

"I thought it was a good idea for you to have your grandmother even if it was at a distance. I wanted you to be happy. You were always happier with her than me."

"I'm sorry, Mom. I love you too, you know."

"I know, dear. But you did need your grandmother to teach you things that I couldn't. At least I didn't think I could. But now I know that I have the same powers as you both do but was afraid to use them in front of your father. He wouldn't understand such things."

"Now that we have hashed everything out, what are you going to do in your new life, Carla?"

"I don't know yet. It is too soon to tell. I don't know what Arnold is going to do. He may not give me the divorce."

"He will not have a choice, dear. If you need me to convince him I will."

"No, Mother. I don't think you should get in the middle of this. He dislikes you enough already."

"Yes, that he does," she laughed to ease the tension in the room.

"Gramma Grace, how do you keep so upbeat and relaxed during this stressful time?"

"Oh, sweetheart, you can do it too. All you have to do is take a deep cleansing breath and wipe him out of your mind. He is toxic and shouldn't be part of your life anymore. Your mother has taken the first steps to a better life without him. You should do the same. I plan to stay here until you both realize that you don't need him and never did."

"I know what you are saying is true, Gramma Grace, but it will be difficult to erase him completely. I wouldn't be here without him."

Carla and Grace exchanged quick looks and turned away so that Athena wouldn't see their concern.

Athena had noticed something wasn't right but didn't ask what the problem was.

"Now about our sleeping arrangements, ladies. I see that you only have one bedroom here. I can get a room at the hotel and you can go with me, Carla. We should leave Athena to her bedroom and not infringe upon her life any further."

"No, I want you both to stay here at least tonight. If you feel you want to go elsewhere afterwards, that's up to you. I want you here so we can have a girls' night out or in. I was planning on having popcorn junk food and movies tonight. Sorry, Mom. You have to live it up a little."

"I wanted to treat you both to dinner. Do you still want to do that? Or, we can order in and I will pay," Gramma Grace announced with a wide smile while dancing a little jig.

Athena and her mother both broke out in giggles at her antics.

"Are you ready for our first girls' night in, then?" Athena asked as she looked at the two women in her life who she treasured.

"Sounds good to me!" Carla proclaimed with delight. "I never eat junk food. It's about time I start!"

"That's great, Mom! How about you Gramma?"

"You don't have to ask me twice, Athena. Where should we order? I love Chinese, Italian, and Greek or just about anything."

"I'm game for any of those too!" Carla jumped in with a chuckle.

Athena smiled and sighed happily watching her mother and grandmother getting along so well after years being apart. She felt so much love bursting inside her and a deep relief for once without her father's angry face dominating their lives.

Later that evening after dinner, which was a combination of Chinese, Italian and Greek choices, everyone was sated. They sat leisurely sipping glasses of wine while looking through the DVDs of movies that Athena had laid out on the coffee table.

They couldn't make up their minds to see just one and chose two comedies – Bridesmaids and Book Club both about strong women.

A little while later they put in the first movie while Athena popped some corn and pulled out the chocolate candies and other goodies for them to choose from.

They shared many belly laughs during and in between the movies. They had stuffed themselves with popcorn and candy and felt closer than they had for a long time.

Athena brought out ice cream and some cookies for dessert. Her mother and grandmother groaned and shook their heads and put up their hands to push Athena's offers away.

"We are stuffed, honey. But thank you for everything. It was a wonderful time. I think we all needed these laughs. I feel so much better," Carla smiled and threw her daughter a kiss.

"Yes, most definitely, it was a perfect girls' night in, Athena. Thank you. We should do this every so often when we need to laugh," Gramma Grace reiterated with a happy sigh.

"Sounds good to me, Mom and Gramma Grace. You are welcome to do this again real soon."

"Now, what are our sleeping arrangements, honey," Gramma Grace asked as she tried to stifle a yawn.

"I'll sleep on the pullout in the living room. You can use my bed. I even have a twin blowup bed if you would rather have your own beds."

"Why don't you use the blowup in the bedroom, Athena, and sleep next to us? I am used to sharing a bed with your grandfather and before that with my sisters."

"Are you sure? I don't mind using the couch."

"No, we want to keep this girls' night going until tomorrow morning. Get your jammies on, girls. We have more talking to do," Gramma Grace announced with a giggle.

Athena pulled out the twin blowup bed, prepared it and lay it next to her queen-sized bed. She didn't know another time in her life that she felt so happy to be with her mother and her grandmother at the same time. They were always at each other's throats and never agreed on anything until now.

When they were finally all done talking like school kids they fell asleep. Athena slept through the night without nightmares or any disturbances.

But there was one person who did not sleep but instead planned to do harm to those he felt had wronged him.

CHAPTER FIFTEEN

Arnold Stone didn't sleep a wink. He was too busy planning what he wanted to do to his wife and daughter. He never expected Carla to file for a divorce after thirty years.

He couldn't believe that she filed for a restraining order too which put him in jail for hours until his lawyer could get him out. She wouldn't get away with this. What did she think she was doing?

He had stayed away three days this time with his woman. She was getting impatient and wanted him to marry her. He never told her that he was already married and had a daughter. Well, now it looked like he would be a free man, but did he want to marry again? No, absolutely not and he wouldn't let Carla marry anyone else either if he had anything to say about it.

His lawyer had told him to lay low until he could get him out of this restraining order. Luckily Arnold was not registered as an abusive husband no matter what Carla claimed. She never reported to the police about her husband's previous abuse.

What Arnold didn't remember was the time Dr. Nettles photographed Carla's injured arm multiple bruises over her back and threatened to give it to the police if he ever harmed her again.

***

Back at Athena's, her mother and grandmother were busy in the kitchen making a large breakfast fit for a lumberjack. She set the table and hummed a tune as they both joined in. It was a happy threesome until there was a banging on the front door.

The three stopped what they were doing and looked at each other. Athena picked up her cell walked toward the window and looked out. She quickly called the police.

Her father was standing there banging and yelling "Open up now, Carla. I know you are there! Athena, let your mother go home where she belongs."

Athena reported to the police that her father was back again. They promised to be there shortly. She responded to her father's taunting, "No, Dad, I will not let Mom go home with you. She doesn't belong there and never did. Leave now or else end up in jail again. The police are on their way."

"You'll be sorry Athena. Carla, this is not the last you will see me. I will be back."

Athena hugged her mother and said, "Don't worry, Mom. He will not harm you anymore. You need to contact your lawyer and tell him the trouble you are having with Dad. Maybe there is something else that can be done or at least try to hurry up the divorce."

"I don't know if he can expedite the divorce because it will be contested. You know your father will not let me go easily."

"I know, Mom. I was afraid of this."

Gramma Grace was quietly listening to them but finally spoke up, "I think we will have to take matters into our own hands, Carla. I know you never wanted to do things my way. But, sometimes my way is the only sensible way to do things safely."

"Mother, I don't want you in the middle of this. He will have to consent because I won't give up."

"How long do you want to be chained to this man, Carla? He will never consent. He will continue to keep you and never let you go."

Carla sighed, "You may be right, Mother. What do you want to do?"

"Let me take care of him, dear. First, let's eat this delicious breakfast. I'm starving."

Athena chirped in, "Me too, Gramma Grace. We'll feel a lot better after we eat. Then you can tell us what you plan to do."

They sat over coffee and waited to hear more about what Gramma Grace wanted to do. During this time the police came and took Arnold away once again and apologized for the disturbance which made the women chuckle, as if Arnold's behavior was their fault.

"Listen, my dears, I don't want to share exactly how I am going to remedy this situation. But, I will tell you one thing. I am going to book a room at a swanky hotel for us, Carla. That way he won't know where you are. Maybe you should come too, Athena. Otherwise, he will keep coming back here to annoy you."

"No, I'm fine here, Gramma Grace. Once he knows Mom isn't here he will leave and try to find her. He doesn't want me."

"Maybe, but he could threaten to harm you to get at your mother."

"No, I don't think he will. I can call the police if he comes back. Also, I'll tell Justin and Dr. Nettles. They will keep an eye on me here."

"I didn't even think of calling Dr. Nettles. He will wonder where I am. I was supposed to go see him to follow up with the therapy on my wrist since it was injured. It's still bothering me a little."

"Well, now is the time to call him, Mom." Athena handed her the cell. "Did Dad hurt you again, Mom?"

"No, it's from the time it was broken. It aches me and therapy sometimes helps."

"Oh. Okay, Mom. Better call the doctor."

Carla's face blanched but nodded as she called the doctor's number.

Gramma Grace pulled Athena into the bedroom to talk to her and give Carla some privacy.

"What's wrong, Gramma?" Athena observed the troubled look on her face.

"Oh nothing, dear. I think your mother needs some time to explain to the doctor what happened. I'm sure she will get quite emotional reliving it all."

"Well, there is nothing that we don't know so far. Right?"

"Sure, dear. But let's sit here and talk about you and your boyfriend, Justin."

"Oh, umm. Okay."

"You didn't think I picked up on that, did you? You changed the subject quickly after mentioning his name to us. You thought since we are getting older we would get distracted easily."

"No, I…"

"That's okay, dear. Your mother didn't pick up on it because her mind was elsewhere. But not me – I don't miss a thing."

Athena giggled and began to tell her about her latest dinner with Justin and how much she cared for him.

A half hour later Carla came looking for them in the bedroom. Her eyes were red and her face was flushed.

"Are you okay, Mom?" She didn't mention that she had only left a message for Dr. Nettles but instead explained, "Yes, honey. I'm fine. Dr. Nettles offered a room for all of us at his beach house in Ralston, New Hampshire. He fears for our safety. He knows how temperamental Arnie can be." Carla didn't want her daughter to know that she had been to the doctor's beach house before.

She also had been told on numerous occasions by Dr. Nettles that she was welcome to use this house in case she felt in need of getting away from Arnold.

"That's nice of him, Mom. Why don't you and Gramma go there? I'm fine here. I'll call Justin and tell him what's going on?"

"Justin? What about this Justin? Why haven't you told me about him? Why didn't you introduce me to him yet?"

"Mom, you know why. It's because of Dad. I didn't want him to judge Justin like he did with Brian. Did he hurt Brian in any way, Mom?"

Carla looked shocked as she stuttered to explain, "Nooooo, no, I don't think he did, dear. I don't know."

Athena gasped in alarm, "You don't know, Mom? What happened to him? You have to tell me."

"Nothing happened to him, Athena, as far as I know."

"But he suddenly disappeared. He was supposed to meet me after his football practice. He didn't even show up for the practice either. No one seemed to know where he was. I know it's been a long time since high school but it always bothered me not to know what happened."

"I'm sorry dear. Your father didn't say anything except that he was not right for you. I don't think he would have harmed him in any way. I know how he can be with his temper though. But he promised not to hurt him. He said he was going to talk to him, that's all."

"He talked to Brian? When?"

"I don't know when, Athena. He didn't tell me that."

"Mom, he must have done something to him. Why didn't he ever call me and explain why he didn't meet me?"

"That, I don't know, honey. Maybe he decided not to see you anymore on his own or your father may have threated to harm him if he did."

"No, I don't think Brian would do that. He would have at least explained that to me. Dad must have convinced him to go away. Maybe he paid him off."

"That is possible, honey. Maybe he did," Carla sighed heavily wanting to change the subject. "Athena, I think we should all go to Dr. Nettles' beach house today before your father comes back again."

Gramma Grace sensed the tension in the air and spoke up, "Yes, I agree. That is the perfect solution to avoid any more confrontations with Arnold, Carla. Good idea. Hopefully Arnold doesn't know where this beach house is."

"No, mother, he doesn't. We were never invited there," Carla responded in a serious tone.

"Well, that's good to know. Let's think positively now, ladies. No more negative thoughts. Okay?" Gramma Grace announced in an upbeat manner.

Athena forced a smile and nodded. "I agree, Gramma. We have to think positively. I still think that I am safe here but I want you both to go to the beach house. Dad won't bother me if he knows Mom is not here."

Gramma Grace shook her head, "No I don't agree with you, Athena. I think your father will try to do something to hurt your mother. One thing he can do is attack you in some manner to get at your mother. He knows how she feels about you. You are her whole life."

"I understand, Gramma. But, I won't let him in. If he does come back I will call the police. I'll also have the protection of Dr. Nettles and Justin."

"Honey, they can't be here all the time to protect you. The police won't be able to protect you either since there is no restraining order against your father from you."

Athena sat down on the couch and hung her head. "I didn't think of that. Maybe I better come with you. I don't want you and Mom to worry about me."

"That's my girl!" Gramma Grace chuckled in relief as she nodded at Carla.

"Thank you, honey. I would feel much better knowing that you are with us," Carla said with a smile and a squeeze of Athena's hand.

"I guess I better start packing." Athena left the living room and hurried to pull out her suitcases. She picked out several outfits, sweaters, a couple of dresses, skirts, tops and scarves, jeans, shorts and shoes. She placed some of her favorite jewelry into a zippered case along with her makeup. She didn't know how long she would be at the beach and wanted to be prepared for anything. She even grabbed a couple of swimsuits and flip flops. While the weather was still warm she planned to spend some time on the beach and take in sun, sand and surf.

Athena rolled out her suitcases and placed them alongside her mother's and grandmother's near the front door. She looked over at her mother and grandmother smiled and took a deep breath.

"Are you sure you packed enough, Athena?" her grandmother asked with a chuckle.

"Umm, I think so." She smiled back at them and giggled. "I may have overdone it a little, huh?"

"Maybe just a tad, sweetheart," Gramma Grace stated with a wide grin.

"Don't worry, honey. Dr. Nettles has a large beach house with four bedrooms, four bathrooms, large living area, kitchen and dining room that are open concept. There are plenty of closets and storage space too. It's right on the beach but he also has a swimming pool with saltwater and a cabana."

"Wow that sounds incredible, Mom. But how do you know all this?"

Her mother didn't answer right away and sat still and looked at her folded hands in her lap. "I...I mean Dr. Nettles told me all about it."

Gramma Grace observed her daughter in silence with a slight smile. "Well, it does sound wonderful! I think we are going on a nice vacation, ladies. This calls for a celebration. Do you have any wine we can bring with us, Athena?"

"Yes, I can bring along a couple of bottles. It's a little early to begin now, Gramma Grace."

"It's never too early, dear. But I can wait until we get there. I'll pack the car. Who's driving?"

Athena raised her hand. "I will. Mom's car is in the garage and will stay there. If Dad looks in there he will think she is still here. I don't think he knows what kind of car I have now."

"Okay, sounds good to me. Let's go, ladies. Times a wasting and I am getting thirsty," Grace giggled like a schoolgirl.

Carla and her daughter couldn't help but laugh at her attitude. Grace didn't look or act like she was 75."

They were almost at the beach when Athena remembered something. "Oh no, I just remembered I have an appointment with Dr. Jasper. What time is it, Mom?"

"It's 2:30 pm, honey. What time is your appointment?"

"It's at 4:00 pm. I need to drop you both off and head back. I should make it in time."

"No, dear. Why don't you call Dr. Jasper and reschedule? Tell him that you have a visitor from out of state, your grandmother, and want to spend time with her."

"I guess I could do that, but, I need to talk to him about what has happened with Dad. It might make me feel better to hash it all out."

"Well, that's up to you, Athena. Whatever you want to do. Up ahead, that's the place," Carla announced in an excited manner.

Athena turned into the spacious driveway of a large white cape with black shutters and opened up the trunk to take out their suitcases. They each grabbed a suitcase and headed to the front door.

Grace went back for the last suitcase and two bottles of wine. She planned on opening one of the bottles and beginning her vacation early.

Athena made sure they were settled after her mother found the key buried in a large flower pot on the front porch and opened the door.

"Honey, go ahead. We will be fine. Your grandmother is going to open one of the bottles and we will be sipping wine and sitting here waiting for you to return so we can go out to dinner. Drive carefully. See you soon."

"Okay. Don't drink too much or you will both be unable to go out at all," Athena laughed as she turned to look at them clinking their glasses and sipping her favorite wine already.

"Cheers, sweetheart. See you soon," Gramma Grace said as she raised her glass.

Athena waved goodbye and hurried to her car. It would take an hour to get back. She wasn't sure where his office was and had to call to get directions. As soon as she added them to her GPS system she was on her way.

CHAPTER SIXTEEN

"How are you doing, Athena?" Dr. Jasper asked once she settled back in the chair across from his desk.

"I'm doing well. But a lot has happened since I last saw you."

"I see. Please explain but take your time."

Athena went through her mother's pending divorce, restraining order, what she dreamt about her father's abuse toward her mother, and how he came to her house looking for her mother.

"Why do you think you forgot all this, Athena?"

"I don't know. I guess maybe it was the stress I felt at that time." She neglected to mention that she thought it was her mother's doing when she touched her forehead to wipe the memories aside. If she mentioned this he would surely think she was insane or going in that direction.

"Have you asked your mother about this abuse?"

"Yes, we spoke of it recently. She said she denied all those times that he ever hurt her to protect me from my father. She feared that he would hurt me too if I tried to fight back for her. She thinks that the shock of seeing her injuries must have made me forget about the abuse."

"Do you think she was correct in assuming that you would fight for her?"

"Yes, I think I would have. At the time I believed her but on the other hand I could see that she couldn't possibly keep hurting herself so violently."

"Did your father ever threaten you over the years?"

"Not really. But he did make it clear to me that he expected me to obey him when he told me to do something, especially about what time to come home at night."

"I see. Were you afraid of him as a young child?"

"Yes. I didn't like it when he raised his voice. It frightened me. He always yelled instead of talking softly to me or my mother. He was always angry and impatient no matter what either of us did."

"Did you feel safe and loved in your home as a child?"

"That's a strange thing to ask me, Doctor. I...I guess I didn't. I never felt love in our home between my parents. But, I knew my mother loved me. She always told me though she didn't always hug or kiss me especially around my father. He didn't like any signs of affection being shown."

"Do you love your father?"

Athena looked down at her hands in her lap before answering, "No, I do not love him. Especially since I now see what kind of man he is. He hurt my mother too many times."

"Do you love your mother?"

"Yes, I do very much. I love her more than ever now that I realize what was going on all these years under my nose. I want to protect her. I want to see my father go to jail for what he has done to her." Athena choked up and couldn't go on.

"Take your time, Athena. It's okay. He can't harm you or your mother now with the restraining order."

"I don't know about that. We had to leave my house and go to another place to get away from him. If we had stayed at my house he would keep coming back and somehow hurt her again. I couldn't have that. My grandmother is here now too. The three of us are at this place safe and sound."

"Your grandmother is here? Did she know about the abuse all these years?"

"Yes. She left because my father drove her away. He never got along with her. She doesn't like him either," Athena said with a nervous giggle.

"How old were you when your grandmother left?"

"I was only five years old. I missed her so much but she talked to me often and that made me feel better."

"Talked to you – do you mean she called you?"

"Umm, yes. That's what I mean. She called me often. We were very close. I was only happy when she talked to me." Athena avoided the doctor's eyes so that he wouldn't see she was not completely truthful.

"I see. So, she was the one stable thing in your upbringing?"

"Yes, she was. I loved her more than my parents at that time. I still love her so much but now that I realized what my mother had to endure I love my mother even more. My mother and I are getting closer now that she is away from my father."

"That's good to know, Athena."

"Are you still having nightmares about an accident like when I saw you in the hospital?"

"Yes, I have had a couple more. These were a little different though."

"What do you mean, different?"

Athena explained that the characters in her dream kept changing the driver from Justin driving to her father and added her mother as a passenger.

"Are you ever in the driver's seat, Athena?"

"No. But I must have been when I was in the accident. There was no one else in the car. The police said there was no evidence of anyone else being involved. I must have skidded in the rain. But I don't know where I was going."

"You may finally remember one day. If you want, I can put you under hypnosis to find out. Would you want to do that?"

"Well, I don't know. I'm not sure. What if it is something that I don't want to know?"

"That's okay, Athena. We don't have to do that. If and when you are ready, please let me know. Okay?"

"Okay. Can I leave now? My mother and grandmother are waiting for me."

"Sure. I was just going to tell you that your time is up. Before you leave please make another appointment with my secretary for next week. I would like to see you once a week unless you need to see me more."

"All right, Dr. Jasper. Thank you."

"Stay safe, Athena. Call me if you need me for anything." Dr. Jasper reached out his hand to Athena and gave it a firm, warm shake.

Athena responded with a smile and nod and left his office. His secretary handed her an appointment card and soon she was on her way back to her family. She felt better after talking to the doctor but at the same time was anxious to get back to her mother and grandmother. She was worried that somehow her father would find them.

She was almost at the beach when her cell rang. She glanced at it in the holder and pressed the speaker button. It was Dr. Nettles.

"Athena, are you okay? I've been trying to reach your mother. Are you at the beach now?"

"No, I just came from Dr. Jasper's office. I had my first appointment with him. I'm on my way back to the beach house now. I dropped my mother and grandmother off first then went to my appointment."

"Okay. I was getting worried. Doesn't your mother have her cell phone with her?"

"No, I don't think she does. But I will make sure to get one for her. She can't go back to the house to get it. She said she was going to call you from your place."

"Oh. Maybe she did try to reach me. I have been doing rounds and didn't look at my messages yet. That's true. She can't go back to her house. It's not safe. I can pick up a cell phone for her if you want and bring it up there after office hours."

"Okay, that sounds good. If it's not too much trouble. You can go out to dinner with us. What time can we expect you?"

"No trouble at all. About 7:00 or maybe a little earlier if I can cancel my last appointment somehow. I am worried about you both. I know how your father can be. He won't give up looking for you either."

"I know. I was thinking the same thing, Doctor. He is persistent."

"There will be no way he can find you. He doesn't even know I have a beach house. I never mentioned it to him. Your mother knew about it though."

"She did? Did she ever go there?"

Dr. Nettles was quiet and didn't answer her question. Instead, he changed the subject and ended the call by saying, "I'll see you all later tonight. Take care."

Athena frowned and pushed the button to shut off the speaker and call. She drove for another half hour and pulled into the driveway of the beach house. As she prepared to knock on the door, her grandmother opened it and smiled at her, clearly having had a little too much to drink. Her mother was sitting on the large couch and laughing as she continued to sip wine.

"Darling, how are you? So happy you came back so quickly. We've missed you, haven't we, Mother?"

"Oh yes, that we did. Miss you, that is," Gramma Grace giggled and wobbled her way back to the couch.

Athena shook her head and scolded them, "You two have had more than enough to drink. You can barely keep your eyes open. Why don't we have something to eat like cheese and crackers? We have to get you both sober before Dr. Nettles comes."

"What? Dr. Nettles is coming here?" her mother asked clearly upset.

"Yes, he called me. He was worried about us and couldn't reach you on your cell phone. You didn't bring it with you?"

"No, I forgot it at home. I was in a hurry to get out before your father got back. Sorry, dear. But why is Dr. Nettles coming? I did call him earlier and left a message that we were here at his house."

"I thought you spoke to him. You were all upset afterward."

"I get upset just talking about it. He didn't answer so I left a long message about everything that has happened."

"Oh. You do know that you will have to tell him all over again. He didn't see your message."

"Oh dear. I hope he reads it. I don't want to go over all that again," Carla sighed.

"To answer your question, Mom, the doctor is bringing you a new cell phone so he can keep in touch with you."

"Oh, I see. It was stupid of me to forget it." Looking at her mother and daughter she excused herself and went to the bathroom to sober up and change before the doctor came.

Gramma Grace chuckled and patted Athena's hand. "Your mother doesn't seem too happy that the good doctor is coming. That is a surprise."

"A surprise? What do you mean, Gramma Grace?" Athena furrowed her brow at her.

"Well, you know that your mother really respects the doctor and doesn't want to make a bad impression on him in her state."

"Yes, I imagine he would not be too happy to see her like this especially with my father and his persistent hunt for her."

Athena went to the refrigerator and pulled out some cheddar cheese and rummaged for crackers. She set up a plate and called her mother to have some.

"I'm coming, dear. Almost ready. I had to throw some cold water on my face and fix my makeup after it smeared and change my dress that was all wet. I was a mess. Sorry about that. We got carried away with the wine and finished the bottle. I guess I needed to unwind a little."

"Unwind a little, Carla? You are as loose as an old mattress that has lost its spring."

"Thanks, Mother. I appreciate your evaluation of me. You aren't too much better right now either."

"Yes, I agree, Carla. I am not a good influence on you. I encouraged you to have more when I knew you had enough. I think we both needed it though. Feeling a lot better now, right?" Grace grinned at her daughter and wiggled her eyebrows in amusement.

"I guess so, Mother. But now let's have a little snack before the doctor comes. What time is he coming, Athena?" her mother asked, anxiety edging her voice.

"He said he would come after office hours around 7:00 or earlier. I invited him to come out with us to dinner. Did you make a reservation anywhere?"

Mother and grandmother stopped eating and exchanged puzzled looks with one another. "No, we forgot. I guess we will have to find some place right away. It's almost 6:00."

Before they could scroll through the internet for a place Athena's phone rang. It was Dr. Nettles.

"Oh, Dr. Nettles. Is everything okay? Are you going to be late?"

"No, I am almost there now. I just wanted to tell you that I made reservations at my favorite Italian restaurant for 7:00. Do you have a reservation anywhere?"

"Umm, no. We were just trying to do that now. That's perfect. We'll be ready when you get here."

Athena ended the call and announced he was on his way and had made a reservation for them. The three woman rushed to the bathrooms to put finishing touches on makeup and hair before he got there.

Everyone was ready as the doorbell rang and Athena went to answer it. Dr. Nettles stood there looking quite handsome with his silver hair brushed and a freshly pressed suit and tie knotted perfectly.

"Come in, Dr. Nettles," Athena said as she stepped aside for him.

"Hello ladies. How are you all doing? I brought a phone for you, Carla. It's important that you keep in touch with the police if there is a problem. I'm just a phone call away also."

Carla walked toward the doctor and accepted the phone. "Thank you, Doctor, for being so thoughtful. It was neglectful of me not to remember to bring my phone."

"That's all right now. I don't want you to go back there. It's too dangerous."

"I know. I don't plan on returning until we need to sell the house and pick up the rest of my stuff." Carla leaned closer to the doctor and whispered, "Did you read my message?"

"Yes, I did, Carla. We will talk more about this later. Don't worry. Okay?"

"Thank you. You are a good friend."

"Good. I'm glad to hear that. Well, ladies, are we ready to go out to dinner? I think you are going to love this place. They have the best calamari and homemade pasta and meatballs."

"Mmm, sounds good to me," Grace announced as she grabbed her sweater off the couch and joined the others at the door.

The restaurant was crowded but the doctor managed to reserve a table overlooking the ocean in a quiet area away from other tables. A bottle of Chianti was brought to the table and decanted as they nibbled on crusty bread and black and green olives.

They ordered their meals and drank more wine as they talked about everything that was happening in the world. Dr. Nettles tried to help them all relax and not think about Arnold.

A short time later their food arrived and they were quiet while they ate with a few remarks about how delicious everything was.

Turning toward Athena Dr. Nettles asked, "How was your appointment with Dr. Jasper."

Athena swallowed a mouthful of pasta and dabbed her lips before responding, "I felt very good and more relaxed after talking to him."

"That's good. That's what I had hoped would happen. I don't want you to share anything with me. I just wanted to know if Dr. Jasper is helping you."

"Yes, I think he is. He's a nice guy too. I feel comfortable with him and able to tell him anything."

"That's wonderful, don't you think so, Carla?"

Carla had eaten most of her food and was on her third glass of wine since she left the beach house and was feeling quite sleepy. She looked up at the doctor and nodded. "Yes, I think it seems he is doing a good job. Thank you for taking care of my daughter. I owe you a lot for all you have done for us over the years."

Grace raised her eyebrows as she observed Dr. Nettles getting a little uncomfortable at what her daughter shared with him. She interrupted, "Carla, dear. I think you have had enough wine for the night. Why don't we order some dessert and coffee?"

"Yes, that sounds perfect, Grace. I agree. They have wonderful Crème Brule." He smiled at Grace and shared a nod with Carla.

"I guess you're right, Mother. I did have a little too much wine. Coffee and dessert sound delicious."

"Yes, I agree, Mom. I would love to try some of that Crème Brule."

She watched her mother who kept her eyes glued on the doctor and smiled when he looked her way. He appeared a little uncomfortable but did not turn away from her gaze.

Gramma Grace poked Athena and asked her about her boyfriend just to change the subject and get her to look away from her mother and the doctor.

"How's the boyfriend, Athena? Does he know where you are now?"

"No, I will have to call him. I didn't get to tell him where I am yet. We are supposed to go out to dinner this weekend."

After dessert and coffee the doctor made sure that he told the waiter to bring him the check.

"Thank you, ladies, for a lovely evening. I hope you enjoyed dinner."

"It was wonderful, Dr. Nettles," Carla gushed still feeling a little woozy.

"Yes, it was delightful, Doctor. Thank you for setting up this reservation. Now let's split this bill four ways," Grace said in appreciation.

Dr. Nettles shook his head and paid the bill before the ladies could take it from the waiter.

Athena added her thanks and looked at her mother who was about to fall asleep. "We both thank you too, Dr. Nettles. It was delicious."

"You are all welcome. It was my pleasure to have dinner with such beautiful ladies. I don't get to have dinner with women. I am getting up in age and don't date since my wife died many years ago."

"It's never too late, Doctor," Grace announced with a chuckle.

CHAPTER SEVENTEEN

The drive back to the beach house was short but everyone was full and tired from all the wine and food.

Athena thanked the doctor and invited him in for another coffee or more wine or mixed drinks.

"No thank you, Athena. I need to get back home. I have an early morning appointment and some surgery scheduled. It was a lovely night. Thank you all. If you need me, don't hesitate to call. There should be plenty of food in the fridge and everything you need in the bathrooms too. I have a maid who comes in twice a week to clean and refill my refrigerator. I will let her know that you are here. Don't want to shock her when she comes and finds you all here."

Carla walked the doctor to the door and whispered, "Thank you, Ash, for a lovely night. The food was spectacular and the view was too. I think you have done more than enough already. We can't stay here forever. I will call my lawyer tomorrow and see what he has to say about the divorce. As soon as Arnold signs the papers we will be leaving here."

"That's not necessary, Carla. You are welcome to stay here as long as you need a place. I would worry less about you if you were here."

"We'll talk some more. I will call you. Okay?"

"Okay. Good night, Carla." Turning to the other women the doctor said, "Good night ladies."

Athena and Gramma Grace said in unison, "Good night, Doctor. Thank you again."

"My pleasure," Dr. Nettles bowed as he opened the door and left.

Carla stayed at the door and watched him until he pulled away. She turned with a sad look on her face and stared at her mother and daughter who were studying her closely.

"What? What are you both looking at?"

"Are you okay, Mom?" Athena queried with a concerned look. "You look a little sad."

"I'm fine, dear. Why are you asking? I know I had too much to drink tonight. Is that what you are worrying about? I'm much better now after the coffee. It was nice of Dr. Nettles to treat us to dinner. He is a thoughtful man," Carla sighed with a smile.

"Yes, he is a lovely man, Carla." Gramma Grace announced as she laid her head back on the couch and sighed contentedly.

Athena looked at her mother and grandmother and sighed in exasperation. "What's up with you two? Are you both falling for Dr. Nettles?"

"Oh, honey. Don't be silly. He is a nice man who I have known for many years. He is a good friend, that's all. I am still married by the way in case you forgot."

"Okay, I understand. Sorry, Mom. I like him too. I feel comfortable around him and can ask him anything. I only wish my own father was as kind and caring."

Carla exchanged quick looks with her mother and said hurriedly, "I think it's time for me to go to bed. I didn't realize how tired I really am. I guess I better watch the booze."

"Yep, I think that would be a good thing to do. I need to do the same things. Watch the booze and go to bed," Grace chuckled.

"Goodnight, Athena. Maybe we can do something fun tomorrow like go down to the beach or shopping and tasting some of the delicious seafood in the little restaurants," Carla added with a yawn.

"Sounds good to me, Mom. Goodnight to both of you. Sleep well. I'm going to stay up a little and read. See you in the morning."

Athena sat in a comfortable chair and pressed buttons to extend the footrest. She sighed and felt, for once, happy and comfortable. She picked up her book on the table and settled down to read until she got sleepy.

Her phone began to ring and she looked around for it. She had left it in her pocketbook which was on the couch across the room. She pushed buttons on the chair to set it down and jumped up to answer her cell.

She didn't recognize the number but answered anyway.

"Hello. Yes, this is Athena Stone."

"I hope I am not calling too late. My boss asked me to call you but I didn't get to until now. Sorry, I am going on too much. I'm calling from Forester Daily to set up an appointment for your interview. You filled out an application for a position with us."

"Umm." Athena had forgotten about that and cleared her throat before speaking again.

"Yes, I did."

"My supervisor, Mr. Forester, will be interviewing you. Are you available on Friday at 2:00?"

Athena pulled up her calendar and made a note. "Yes, I can make that."

"All right. See you on Friday at 2:00, Athena."

"Thank you so much. I look forward to it."

"Good night. I apologize for the lateness. Please don't tell my boss. I may lose my job."

"No problem. My lips are sealed. What is your name?"

"Mark. My name is Mark. Thank you, Athena, for understanding. I am still working and have a few more things to do before I can leave."

"Wow, you are working really late. Do you do that often? Will I have to do that if I get the job?"

"Yes, I do. About your position, I can't say. Well, I've got to go. See you on Friday, Athena. Thank you again."

"Okay. See you then, Mark."

Athena looked at her watch and saw how late it was – 9:00 pm was a little late for a call from a company. She picked up her book but couldn't get into it. She went to her bedroom and pulled out her laptop and printer. She scanned for her resume and reviewed it. She printed it out after connecting to the doctor's computer and printer and placed it on her nightstand in a folder. She couldn't believe she had forgotten about sending her resume to this company. It was over a month ago. When she didn't hear back from them she had put them out of her mind.

She got ready for bed as she thought over what she would say at her interview in a few days. Maybe things were finally looking up for her.

She closed her eyes and was soon sleeping soundly. There were no dreams that she could remember the next morning and she felt refreshed for the first time in a long time.

She got up from bed and opened up the curtains and windows to a beautiful, sunny day. She could hear voices in the kitchen as she headed that way.

"Good morning, sleepy head," Gramma Grace chided her.

"What time is it? I didn't oversleep, did I?"

"No, honey. It's only 8:00 am. We just got up a little while ago ourselves. I had the most wonderful sleep. I haven't slept that well in a long time."

"That's great, Mom. I feel the same. I had a good night's sleep too."

"It could be all the wine and good food we had. That knocked us out," Gramma Grace replied with a smile and a wink.

"What smells so good?" Athena came closer to the stove.

"Well, I thought it would be nice to have some of my famous omelets with potatoes, onions, parsley and bacon on the side," Gramma Grace announced.

Carla manned the toaster and set the table. She waved at Athena to put the coffee pot on.

"What kind of coffee do you want? The good doctor has all kinds of coffee for his coffee maker. Caffeine or not?"

"Caffeine for me, dear," her mother said.

"Me too, honey," Gramma Grace stated as she flipped the omelets with precision.

Toast was laid out on plates as Grace placed omelets, potatoes and bacon next to each serving.

Athena brought over cups of steaming coffee and sat down to enjoy the delicious smelling breakfast.

"Thank you so much, Gramma Grace, for this wonderful breakfast. You too, Mom. I know you helped by cooking the bacon and making the toast." She winked at them both.

"Well, you made the coffee, Athena. It was a group effort," her mother said with a smirk.

"Let me do the clean up since I didn't really do much else."

"That's fine. For now, let's enjoy this breakfast," Gramma Grace announced as she shoveled in a mouthful with a sigh.

"It's delicious, Gramma. Thank you. Mom makes omelets like this too. She must have gotten your recipe."

"Yes, I bet she did," Grace laughed as she winked at her daughter.

After breakfast and a second cup of coffee Athena announced that she had received a call last night and had an interview.

"You have an interview, Athena. That's wonderful!"

"Yes, Mom. I had forgotten I had sent in my resume to Forester Daily."

"What kind of company is this?" Gramma Grace asked.

"It's a newspaper – journalist is what I applied for."

"Oh, you will knock the interview out of the park for sure, Athena. No problem there. Once they take one look at you they will fall in love," Gramma Grace stated with a nod to her daughter.

"I agree, honey. They will love you. You are intelligent, confident and beautiful. Of course you will get the job," her mother retorted.

"I know you both think I will get the job but it is not a beauty contest. It is a job. They will look at my resume which doesn't show much in positions since college. I don't think they will be much impressed with me."

"Don't worry too much, Athena. You will do well. I don't want to change the subject, but let's get outside. The weather is beautiful and the water looks perfect," Gramma Grace stated emphatically.

"Okay. Sounds good to me. How about you, Athena?"

"Yes, Mom. Let's get out there. I need to brown up a little. I haven't been out too much lately."

"Okay, one of you grab a beach bag and pack it with towels. I saw one in the spare bedroom. I will pack some sodas and waters in the cooler here and fill it with ice. I can put in some fruit if anyone wants a snack. Let's go!"

"Where does Gramma get all her energy for her age, Mom?"

"I don't know, dear. I certainly don't have as much as she does and never did."

"We better hurry up or she will be coming into our rooms to help us," Athena giggled as she pulled out her bathing suit and cover up.

Out on the beach they laid out a blanket and sighed. Athena set up the umbrella and put the cooler in the shade. She watched her grandmother run down to the water and jump in. She was amazing! She wished she could be as fun loving and energetic as she was.

Her mind went to her upcoming interview. Would she be able to convince them to take her on even if she hadn't worked much in her chosen field yet?

When she heard her mother's voice she snapped out of it.

"What did you say, Mom?"

"You were far away, Athena. What is going on? Are you okay?"

"I'm fine, Mom. I was just thinking about my interview on Friday. I'm a little nervous but I'll be okay."

"Of course you will, honey. I have faith in you. You are stronger than you know."

"Thanks, Mom. I will try to think positively that I will get it."

"That's my girl. Positivity is the way to bring more positive vibes toward you. Negativity wipes out all positivity."

"Makes sense to me, Mom. Thanks. Should we go check out the water? Gramma Grace looks like she is having a good time."

Much later they were exhausted after a long day in the sun and surf. They went back to the house and decided to go to the local beach shops to pick up some souvenirs and then onto the little restaurants to check out the local fish and other seafood for dinner. The end of the summer was near and they wanted to enjoy every minute of it.

They all felt safe and comfy at the beach but how long would it be before that would change?

CHAPTER EIGHTEEN

On the day of her interview Athena had to go back to her apartment to pick up a suit. She hadn't brought one with her. She stayed at home and puttered around the apartment until the time for her interview.

Just before she left she called Justin to let him know what was going on and where she would be staying. However, he didn't answer his phone. She decided to leave a quick message. If she didn't hear back from him later she would call him again. They were going out tomorrow on their second date and she hadn't heard from him all week. He must be extremely busy not to call her all week. She checked her calls and voicemail to make sure she hadn't missed his call.

Being at the beach the past few days was relaxing and fun spending time with her mother and grandmother. She hadn't even thought of Justin until now. What kind of girlfriend was she?

She drove to the Forester Daily and stopped at the desk in the lobby to the office. A handsome young man sat at the desk on the phone and clearly looking stressed and confused. When he finally put down the phone he looked up to see Athena standing there smiling at him.

"Can I help you?"

"Hi, Mark, is it? I'm Athena Stone. I have an appointment for an interview with Mr. Forester at 2:00 pm."

"Hi, Athena. Yes, I'm Mark. How could you tell? Do I look disheveled and out of control?" he chuckled as he shuffled more papers around his desk.

"Not at all. I recognized your voice from our phone call."

"Oh, I see. Let me call Mr. Forester and tell him you are here a little early. He may be able to see you sooner. Please have a seat over there. It's nice to meet you."

"Thank you. It's nice to meet you too."

Athena sat down and looked through the newspapers and magazines that were on the table nearby. She pulled up one that looked interesting as she waited for Mark to let her know if Mr.

Forester was ready for her. She watched Mark as he spoke on the phone and continued to shuffle more papers around his desk clearly confused about something.

Mark spoke up suddenly, "Athena, you can go in now. Mr. Forester is waiting for you at the second door on the right."

"Okay. Thank you, Mark." She gave him a warm smile to help him calm down. He was looking a little more anxious now that he had spoken to his boss.

As Athena walked down the corridor toward the second door on the right, the door opened and a tall, impressive and confident looking middle-aged man came out to meet her. He pushed up his glasses and smoothed his peppered gray hair over his ears.

"Athena? Nice to meet you. I'm Gabe Forester." Reaching out his hand to her, he shook hers firmly and guided her into his office.

"Nice to meet you too, Mr. Forester."

"Please sit down. Would you like some coffee, tea or a soft drink?"

"No thank you. I brought my resume in case you needed a copy."

Mr. Forester reached forward and accepted it. "Thank you. My office manager seems to have mislaid it. He's normally all together but today he is not. I apologize for that."

"I'm sure he is well organized. He was very nice to me on the phone and made me feel comfortable."

"I'm glad to hear that. He's a good man and I wouldn't know what to do without him. But today something is going on. Sorry. Let's get down to your interview. Tell me a little bit about yourself."

Athena told him about her degree in Journalism, how she always wanted to work for a newspaper like Forester Daily. She mentioned that she had a job for a short time as a local reporter in a small newspaper and did some writing for columns in small magazines. She said she had some lesser jobs in between to earn money to keep her solvent until something better came along. She mentioned that she had contemplated being a teacher of writing courses and journalism at one time but nothing came open for her.

After an hour passed and many questions about her knowledge of journalism were asked, Mr. Forester stood up and thanked Athena for her time. They shook hands again and he said, "I will be in touch with you soon, Athena. It was a pleasure to get to know you."

"Thank you, Mr. Forester. It was my pleasure too. I look forward to hearing from you."

Athena passed by Mark's desk and waved in thanks as she smiled at him and left. She wondered why he was so anxious. He must be dealing with some serious stuff. She sighed hoping he was feeling less so the next time she saw him. That's if she was invited back or offered a position.

As Athena was leaving the office a man was running toward her. He stopped abruptly in front of her causing her to jump back in alarm.

"Oh, I'm so sorry. I didn't mean to startle you. I wasn't paying attention to where I was going. Are you all right?"

"Umm, yes I'm fine. Where was the fire?"

"Ha. Yes it appeared that there must have been one the way I was running. Sorry about that again. I'm Lucas Strait. Who may you be?"

"Athena Stone."

"Nice to meet you, Athena. Did you just have an interview?"

"Yes, I did. How did you know that?"

"Well, I knew there was an opening and I saw your name on Mark's desk. Did you think that I was just a good reporter?"

"Are you?" Athena smirked as she looked at this handsome blond-haired man with startlingly beautiful green eyes.

"You are a woman of few words, Athena. That is quite an oddity in itself." Lucas smiled, showing off brilliantly white and perfect teeth.

"Sometimes," Athena chuckled.

"Are you trying to drive me crazy? I can't get much out of you. Would you like to go for a coffee?"

"Maybe." Athena couldn't help herself. She was enjoying teasing this attractive man who evidently was a reporter.

"Listen, Athena. I have to report back to my boss about a story. Can you wait here? I'll be quick. I really would like to take you out for a coffee.

"Okay," Athena smiled as she tried to stifle a giggle.

"That was what I hoped you would say," he laughed heartily as he raced into the office.

Athena waited for ten minutes and was about to leave when Lucas appeared. He pushed back his long blonde hair that was curling in his eyes and smiled. "I'm sorry. Gabe kept me longer than I thought. He is quite a talker when he gets going."

"Yes, I know."

"Is this how it's going to be? Will you ever answer me with more than three words?"

"I don't know."

Lucas took her hand and wound it through his arm as he guided her to his car. They drove a short distance and stopped at a local coffee shop, The Coffee Pot, her favorite place.

The place was packed with a long line. Lucas found a table tucked away in the back and told Athena to wait there while he waited in line. Before he turned away he asked, "What kind of coffee would you prefer, Athena?"

"Decaf with cream only."

"Sure thing. I didn't expect four words this time," he chuckled as he headed toward the growing line.

Athena sat back and smiled as she watched Lucas walk away. He definitely looked good from the back also. She frowned at her thoughts. What was she thinking going out with a strange man? She was seeing Justin. She was about to get up and leave the place, when Lucas appeared with two coffees and cakes.

"That was quick."

"Yes, I have connections. They know me here and how I always need to get my coffees quickly and get out of here."

"Is that so?"

"Athena, who are you?" Lucas flashed his brilliant smile again.

She felt her knees getting weak as she couldn't take her eyes off of him. What was happening here?

"Are you going to answer me?"

"I guess." She sipped her coffee and nibbled on the tasty coffee cake.

"Well, since you won't tell me about yourself, I am forced to talk about myself." He puffed out his chest and winked at her.

Athena couldn't keep from laughing out loud at his antics. She waited to see what he had to say for himself.

"Ah, I see you have a sense of fun in you, even though you have nothing to say." Lucas talked about his background and working at different jobs. After a few more minutes he sat back and sipped his coffee and took a large bite out of his cake as he watched this beautiful woman sip her coffee. He never knew a woman who didn't talk her head off. It was refreshing. He smiled and nodded to her as they sat in solitude without another word spoken between them.

Athena finished her coffee and stood up. "Thank you for the coffee and cake. They were both delicious."

"Wow, many words this time. I'm impressed."

"I have to go. It was nice meeting you, Lucas."

"Okay, but when can I see you again?"

"I don't know. Maybe if I got this job we would work together."

"Yes, you would work with me. The person you would be replacing was my partner on several stories."

"Oh, I see."

"Oh no, back to three words again? I hope when you write, that you use more than three words."

Athena nodded and smiled as she left the shop. She turned once out on the sidewalk and remembered that she came with Lucas.

He was right behind her and took her arm and guided her back to his car. He opened the door for her and let her get settled before closing it.

"I'll take you back to your car, Athena. Did I say something to upset you?"

"No. I need to go."

"Okay. Well, maybe we will see each other again when you get the position."

"That's an 'if.'"

"No. I think it's a given, Athena. Now which car is yours?"

Athena pointed out her car in the newspaper parking lot and thanked Lucas again before walking away. She could feel his eyes on her but she didn't turn around to look at him.

Athena drove out of the lot and thought over all she had discussed with Mr. Forester. She felt confident that she had done a good job in her interview and hoped he thought so too.

But, her meeting with Lucas Strait kept coming into her mind. She couldn't forget his beautiful green eyes, pearly white teeth and easy and likeable manner.

She decided to stay at her apartment since she had a date with Justin the next night. She hoped she would get a good night's sleep so she wouldn't look tired and washed out. She called her mother to tell her that she wouldn't be going back to the beach house.

"Hi, honey," her mother answered.

"Hi, Mom. I won't be going back there tonight. I have a date with Justin tomorrow and wanted to stay home tonight."

"Okay, dear. Is everything all right? Did you get the job?"

"Yes, everything is fine, Mom. I won't know about the job just yet."

"Okay. Well, call us tomorrow after your date when you are heading back here."

"Will do, Mom. Good night."

The next day Athena cleaned her apartment and went through her clothes to see what she would wear for her date. She began clearing out old clothes and got so involved that she lost track of time. She looked at her watch and realized that Justin would be coming in an hour and a half or so.

He did say he could come earlier than 7. She had to hurry and get ready.

She decided to shower first then choose something to wear. Later, as she dressed, she realized that she was starving since she had only had a cup of coffee and a piece of coffee cake for lunch.

Athena put on her finishing touches and sat down to relax until Justin arrived. She scrolled through her phone to see if he had tried to call her. That was strange that he hadn't, especially since she had left him a message.

She looked at her phone and noted the time. It was now 7:15. He was usually early. She calmed herself down and got up and began pacing the floor. She jumped as her phone vibrated in her hands,

She answered expecting to hear Justin's voice but it was her mother.

"Mom, is everything all right?"

"Yes, dear. I thought you had a date tonight with Justin?"

"Yes. I do have a date but he hasn't showed up yet. Why are you calling?"

"I just felt that something was wrong. Are you okay, Athena?"

"Umm, yeah. I'm fine, Mom. It's just that…"

"What? Is your father there?"

"Oh no, Mom. It's not that. It's Justin. He's late. He's never late. Well, the two times we were together he wasn't anyway." Athena sighed.

"He's probably on his way now. Don't worry, honey. Did you hear about the job?"

"I guess so. Thanks, Mom. No. I didn't hear from Mr. Forester yet. But Lucas said I would probably get it."

"Lucas? Who is Lucas?"

"Oh, someone who works there."

"I see. Okay. Well, have a good time tonight. Call us when you get home. We will be up late. Love you, honey. Gramma sends kisses too."

"Kisses and hugs to you both. See you tomorrow."

CHAPTER NINETEEN

Justin was running a little late with all the meetings he had to attend at the last minute. He stopped by the florist to pick up a bunch of roses and headed over to Athena's house. He had seen a couple of calls from Athena but didn't have time to call her. He would see her soon.

As he was rounding the corner before arriving at Athena's, he noticed a car following him a little too closely. He slowed down and waited to see if the car would pass him. It didn't.

Justin pulled over to the side of the road. What's with this guy? Doesn't he know he can pass me now?

He was getting out of the car as the other car stopped behind him. Justin walked up to the car to talk to the person.

The man in the car rolled down the window and looked up at Justin. He said, "I think I am lost. Can you help me?"

The man got out of his car with a map in his hands. He stepped closer as Justin leaned over the map to see what the man was pointing to. As Justin did this the man pulled out a rubber mallet and hit Justin over the head knocking him out. The man caught Justin as he was about to fall and pulled him toward his car. He leaned him against the front door as he opened the back door and pushed and tugged him onto the seat and shut the door.

The man looked around to see if anyone saw what he had done. Feeling safe that no one had seen him do this, he started the car and pulled away.

***

Athena paced the living room and kept looking out the window to see if Justin was coming. She checked her phone but there were no messages. She called his number and waited. It went to voicemail.

Where was he? It's now 7:45! I can't believe that he would not call me to say he was going to be late. Something isn't right. Could he have been in an accident or…? Something must have happened to him.

Before she could stop herself she called her mother's number and tapped her feet until she answered.

"Mom, something has happened to Justin. I know it! He would have called me to let me know he was going to be late!"

"Athena, honey. Slow down. What time was he supposed to arrive?"

"He told me he was coming around 6:30 or 7:00."

"Okay, honey. Relax. Have you tried calling him?"

"Yes, I did, twice already. It goes to his voicemail. That isn't right. He would have his phone with him and always answer or at least call me back."

Carla sighed and looked back at her mother who was shaking her head. "This isn't good, Carla. Arnold must be behind this. Let me ponder on this for a minute."

"What did Gramma Grace say?"

"Nothing, Athena. Why don't you give Justin a little while longer, then try calling him again. Let us know if he does come or if you finally reach him. I'll stay by the phone."

"Okay, Mom. But this isn't right. Do you think Dad has something to do with this?"

"I...I don't know, honey. I hope not. Is there someone else you can call about Justin, his work maybe?"

"No, I don't have the number. I don't even know the name of the place where he works," Athena choked on her words.

"Are you okay, Athena? Do you want us to come over there?"

"No, Mom. If it is Dad that is what he is hoping you will do. He wants you to come to me."

"Do you see his car anywhere on the street?"

"No, but I am going out and riding around to see if it is anywhere close by."

"Okay, honey. Call me as soon as you know something. Be careful."

"I will, Mom. I better go. Talk to you later." Athena put her phone in her pocket and grabbed her purse and keys. She drove around the neighborhood and suddenly stopped when she saw Justin's car on the next street. She jumped hastily out of her car and ran over to his car and peeked in. He wasn't there but a bouquet of roses sat on the front seat and a small black box.

Oh my God! Is that what I think it is? He was here and someone must have stopped him before he got to my house. It must be my father. What can I do? Do I call the police? What will I tell them?

Athena drove back to her house and called her mother again. "Mom, I found Justin's car but no sign of him. He was on his way to my house and had a bouquet of roses and a small black box on the front seat. There's no sign of Dad. What do I do? Should I call the police?"

Carla didn't answer right away but whispered to Grace filling her in what Athena had just said.

"Mom, are you there?"

"Yes, dear. I am here. I was just telling your grandmother what you said."

"What does Gramma Grace think I should do?"

Gramma Grace took the phone away from her daughter and answered, "Honey, don't worry. I am taking care of it. I am going to find your father and see if he has Justin. Sit tight. I will call you back as soon as I know."

"But…Gramma Grace, what are you going to do? You can't go to the house. He is dangerous."

Carla took the phone away from her mother and continued talking to Athena. "It's going to be okay, Athena. Your grandmother is going to check her cards to see where your father is and what he is doing. We will call you back as soon as we know something."

"I don't understand, Mom. How will her cards tell her where he is and what he is doing?"

"Ha ha, only your grandmother knows that. Just be patient, honey. We will know soon enough. Okay? Do you want to come here?"

"No, Mom. I need to stay here in case Justin finally comes."

"I understand. Why don't you have a nice cup of tea and relax. Everything is going to be all right."

"Okay," Athena sighed heavily and put the phone down as she went to the kitchen to make a cup of green tea. She only hoped it would calm her down. She felt her insides jumping all over the place and her mind was creating horrible scenes with Justin being murdered.

She kept thinking over the little back box. Was he going to propose like in my dream?

***

Justin groaned and tried to sit up. He found his hands and feet tightly tied and he was lying in a small space. He couldn't even turn over. He peered into the darkness and realized that he was in the trunk of a vehicle. Who did this to him and why?

Arnold opened up a beer and sat in front of the television to relax. He hadn't decided what he was going to do with this young man who was seeing his daughter. He had seen him go to her house in the past and followed them on their date. They were getting too close. He couldn't have that. He didn't want his daughter to have anyone. She had to be punished and kept without love. This was one way he could get to his wife. If she knows Athena is unhappy she would come forward and help her. It's just a matter of time before Carla surfaces and then he will grab her.

Justin reaches around behind his back and grips a tire iron. He bangs the back of the seats and pushes until he opens up the seats and pushes them forward. He wiggles his way onto the back seats and reaches for the door handle. Luckily it's not locked and turns easily as he falls out of the car. He is in a garage. He looks around to find something that will cut the ties off his hands and feet. He must first move his arms forward under his legs and bring them up so he can stand up. Once upright he searches the shelves and finds a cutting tool to remove his ties.

Arnold feels a bit groggy after his third beer but decides to go and check on his prisoner. He opens the door to the garage and steps down.

Justin is waiting for him and strikes the man down with a hammer. He checks the car for keys. When he comes up empty he rummages through the man's pockets. Luck is with him so far. He opens the garage door and drives away. He doesn't know where he is but calls the police to report his kidnapping. He looks at the house and number and finds the name of the street to tell the police.

What he needs to do now is get far enough away from the man in case he wakes up and comes looking for him. He drives around until he recognizes some streets and eventually gets back to his own car. He stays there and reports to the police what he has done and where they can find him.

Arnold wakes up and sees that his car is gone. He feels the bump on his head. What happened? How did this man get out of the trunk? Where did he go?

He hears a knocking and goes back into his house. When he looks out there are two policemen standing on his front steps. Now what? Did that man call them?

Arnold opens the door and tries to appear surprised that the police are there.

"Arnold Stone? We need to speak with you. We just received a call about a kidnapping here."

"A kidnapping? What kidnapping? There is no one here but me."

"We need to come in and search your house. We will get a warrant if need be."

"Well, then you better get one because you are not coming in here." Arnold slams the door on the officers.

***

Gramma Grace looks over her cards and sees what she expected. She closes her eyes and sends good vibes Justin's way. She feels that he is not out of danger yet. She only hopes that they can get there before something terrible happens.

She turns to her daughter who is waiting to hear something from her. When Carla sees the look of horror on her mother's face she knows that it's not something she wants to share with Athena.

***

Arnold grabs his gun and goes next door to borrow his neighbor's car telling him that it's an emergency. He drives like the maniac that he is to where he last saw this young man. He hoped that he was still there.

When he gets closer he sees his own car and the young man's car and slows down. He parks further back and walks up to the two cars.

Justin lays his head back on the headrest of his front seat and falls asleep unaware that the man who kidnapped him is back.

Arnold sneaks up to the car and peers in. He grips the door handle and pulls it open quickly startling Justin and knocking him to the ground.

He pulls him toward his car once again and ties him up more thoroughly. He dumps him onto the back seat since the trunk is useless. He stuffs a rag into Justin's mouth and drives away. As he is pulling away he sees a police car coming down the street. It heads over to the two cars. He looks away and keeps driving in the opposite direction.

Justin continues to struggle and tries to talk against the rag in his mouth. But stops when the man threatens to kill him if he doesn't be quiet.

Arnold knows he can't go home. He has to find a place to stay until he can get his wife to come. He will exchange this young man for her. He calls his daughter's phone and waits.

Athena grabbed her phone the second it rang when she recognized the number. "Dad, why are you calling me?"

"Athena, how are you? I was just calling to get your mother's phone number. It seems that she did not take her cell with her wherever she went. I need to speak with her. It's urgent and a matter of life and death."

"What do you mean a matter of life and death?" Athena's voice shakes as she tries to keep her hands from dropping the phone.

"I need her number, Athena. If you want your boyfriend to live, you must give me her number. I have a little proposition for her."

"Daddy, please tell me. Did you hurt Justin? Please don't hurt him. What do you want? I will do anything to keep him safe."

"Well, what you need to do is give me your mother's number so I can talk to her. If she comes to me, I will let Justin go."

"No. You can't do that. She won't come to you. If you don't let Justin go, I will call the police."

"Ha, that's funny. Your boyfriend already did that. They are looking but will never find me."

"Please tell me where you are. I'll come to you and you can keep me and let Justin go."

"Why would I want you? You are not even my.... Oh, never mind. I guess I will have to kill him then."

"No, no, please don't do that! Dad, please let him go!"

"Tell your mother what I said, Athena. She will know where I am. It's where I proposed to her. I'll be waiting for her. No police or he will be dead."

"No, please listen to me." The line went silent.

Athena was shaking so badly, she could hardly hold her phone to call her mother.

CHAPTER TWENTY

Athena explained what her father had said about where he would be.

"What did you say, Athena? Oh my God! What are we going to do? Did you call the police?"

"I wanted to talk to you first, Mom. He said Justin already called the police and they are looking for him."

"Well, then we need to call them and let them know he is hiding out. I know where he is."

"No, Mom. He said no police or he would kill Justin."

Gramma Grace listened to what was going on and pressed the speaker on the phone and spoke up, "I will go in place of you, Carla."

"No, Mother. He doesn't want you. He wants me. I have to go. Call the police and let them know where he is after I leave. Give me enough time to get there, though."

"No one is going without me. I will go with you, Mom," Athena announced stubbornly.

"Okay, dear. I will come get you. Tell your father I am on my way and not to hurt the boy."

"All right. Please drive carefully, Mom."

Carla picked up the keys to the car that Dr. Nettles left there for them. Her mother followed her out and grabbed them from her. "You are not going without me. I can talk him out of hurting either one of you. You know I can do that."

"Okay, let's go. But I need to call Dr. Nettles to let him know that we are going out. He will worry if he comes over and we are not here."

"Well, do it on the way. We can't waste time, Carla. A young man's life is in danger. You need to get your life in order, girl. Make up your mind what you are going to do with this doctor. I know you love him."

"This is not the time to talk about such things, Mother. There is plenty of time for that."

"There may not be, dear. Time is running out for all of us."

"Don't talk nonsense, Mother. Just drive and let me call the doctor."

Carla called Dr. Nettles and waited as she felt her whole body tremble and her hands shaking. She explained in detail what had happened.

"Carla, you can't do this. He is dangerous."

"Yes, I know he is dangerous but I need to do this, Dr. Nettles. Please understand. Yes, we will call the police now. They are already looking for Arnold. Justin called them earlier. I am the only one that can save Justin."

"Be careful. I'm coming too. Tell me where this place is."

Carla hesitated but then gave the doctor directions to the place.

***

Athena called her father back and told him her mother was on her way.

She stayed by the window until her mother and grandmother drove up and beeped the horn. Athena ran out and jumped into the back seat. She didn't have a chance to click her belt before her grandmother gunned the engine and raced away to their destination.

"Where are we going, Mom? You said you knew where Dad was."

"Yes, I do. Let me explain. When we first got together before we were married, we went to Camp Winnacut on US23 and stayed in a little cottage overnight. Your father wanted to show me how thoughtful he could be. He ordered a lovely dinner and had flowers all over the room, my favorite, roses. He proposed to me at that cottage. We were married a few days later."

"Oh, I see. He wined and dined you so to speak. Did you love him, Mom?" Athena held her breath as she waited for her mother to respond.

"Not anymore, sweetheart. But I guess I must have in the beginning. It all changed when he…" Carla couldn't go on.

"It's okay, Mom. Don't say anymore. I understand. I think I would feel the same. Maybe something happened to change him."

"Yes, something did, Athena. Your sister died," Gramma Grace interjected.

"But why would Dad become so violent toward you."

"I…I don't know, dear."

"What's wrong, Mom. I know you are keeping something from me. What is it?"

"Carla, you have to explain to her. She deserves to know."

"Not now, Mother. We need to concentrate on getting this young man out of danger."

"But, when are you going to explain all of this cryptic talk? While you think this over I am calling the police and letting them know we are on our way to save Justin."

"No. You can't do that, Athena. Your father will hurt him just to spite us for calling them."

"Listen to your mother, Athena. She knows him better than you do. You have been in the dark for too long. She will explain about this soon. Let's get there. In the meantime, let's decide how we are going to get Justin away from your father and at the same time keep your mother safe."

"All right," Athena conceded.

"I want to go in to talk to him first, Mother. If he sees you and Athena, he might become more agitated."

"Okay, but I will be right behind you if I see that he is not being reasonable. I don't want him to hurt you or Justin."

"He won't hurt Justin if he has me. He will let the boy go. I will insist that he does that."

"Okay, but how do we get you away from him?" Athena asked with a tremor in her voice.

"Don't worry about me, honey. I will be all right. I want you and your grandmother to take Justin away and leave me here with your father. We will work things out. I will talk to him and make him listen to reason."

While Athena was listening to her mother explain, she phoned the police and explained to them in a whisper what was happening and where they were going.

"What are you doing, Athena?" her mother exclaimed in alarm.

"I'm trying to protect you, Mom. I don't want anything to happen to you. I don't trust Dad. The police are on their way to the camp. Let them handle things."

Gramma Grace smiled at Athena and nodded in agreement. "I agree, Carla. Arnold is not the type to listen to reason. Let me go in first and use my powers to influence him to let Justin go. That is the only way you and Justin will be safe. The police may not get here in time. Let me try."

"He could take out his frustrations on you."

"I'll handle him. He will not be able to do anything to me. You underestimate my powers of persuasion."

"No, I don't, Mother. But I think you underestimate Arnold's temper and volatile nature."

Ignoring her daughter's remark Grace announced, "We're here, Carla. Is this the cabin, number seven, on the end?"

"Yes. That's the one."

Grace turned off the engine and touched her daughter's arm. "You stay here with Athena. I will talk to Arnold and bring Justin out with me. Be prepared to drive away as quickly as you can. I would suggest that you get into the driver's seat now, Carla, so you will be ready when I come out."

Before Grace could go into the cabin the police pulled up and came out with guns. They ran up to the cabin and pushed Grace aside.

"We will handle things from here. Please go back to your car. Are you the person who called us?"

"No. That was my granddaughter. It's my son-in-law there with my granddaughter's boyfriend. He is threatening to hurt him and my daughter."

"Please get into your car and drive away. We don't want you to be in the way."

Grace tried to resist but moved away when the police blocked her way to the cabin.

Another car pulled up behind them and Dr. Nettles got out.

"Are you all okay?"

"Yes. We're fine but you shouldn't be here." Carla opened her door to get out to speak with him.

"What are you doing here, Dr. Nettles?" Athena asked.

Before he could answer, a car engine was suddenly heard as Arnold pulled out and nearly ran over the policemen who were standing in the road. He raced away with Justin in the back seat.

The police ran to their cars and swiftly followed Arnold's vehicle.

Grace got into the car and pulled Carla and Dr. Nettles inside and followed closely behind the police. The three women and the doctor held their collective breaths as Grace pushed the car to keep up with the police and Arnold.

"Mother, you are going to kill us all with your reckless driving! Please slow down!" It had begun to rain heavily.

"I can't slow down, Carla. We'll lose them! Who knows what Arnold is going to do? We need to keep up with them."

"Gramma Grace, please stop. We can't do anything even if we catch up with them. We need to stay away. We can't help Justin either. The police will stop Dad and get Justin away."

"Do you really believe that your father will slow down for them to catch him?"

"No, I know he won't but he could get into an accident if the police keep pushing him to go faster." Athena sat up and cried out, "Oh my God! It's my nightmare happening!"

"What? What are you talking about, Athena?" Her mother turned toward her and saw how white her daughter's face had become.

Dr. Nettles patted Athena's hand to calm her down and said, "It's okay, Athena. Don't worry, the police will get him to stop."

She smiled wanly at the doctor and announced in alarm, "It's my dream, Mom. My dream about driving and getting into an accident. I was in an accident."

"Yes, Athena. I remember you were in an accident but your father wasn't involved."

"I know. But…"

Grace slowed down and pulled to the side of the road as she watched the police cars disappear in the distance. She looked back at her granddaughter and asked, "What dream, Athena?"

Athena explained about her dream that Justin was in the car and was killed. She added that she was injured and not in the car but landed on a mound of mud, so the doctors told her. She told her mother about another dream that had her father and Justin in the car with the same outcome. She didn't mention that she had also seen her mother in another version of the dream.

"It was a rainy night and the car took the turn too quickly and went off the road. This happened to me but no one else was in the car. That's why I was in the hospital."

"Of course, honey. I remember, but what does that have to do with your father and Justin?"

"Don't you understand? This is happening now like in my dream. I dreamt this was going to happen. It's happening now in a second!"

An earth shattering crash was heard as everyone jumped in alarm.

***

The police watched as the car went off the road and crashed crushing both the driver and the passenger. They called an ambulance and worked to remove the bodies but it was too late. They were both killed on impact.

The bodies were moved to the morgue as the police worked to identify the bodies so they could notify the next of kin.

The four were still sitting in shock in their car when the police drove up to talk to them. Athena screamed when the police came to their car and reported what had transpired. Dr. Nettles pulled her into his arms and held onto her as she cried.

"I'm sorry, Mrs. Stone, but we need for you to come to the morgue to identify the bodies. Do you know the other person in the car?"

Athena spoke up between fits of crying, "Yes…yes, I know who it is. It's my boyfriend, Justin Dracker."

Gramma Grace nodded to the police and said she would follow them back to the morgue.

Carla and Grace helped Athena into the building to identify the bodies. They were all in shock from what had happened and didn't say a word as the morgue attendant pulled out the tables and uncovered the bodies for them to identify.

Athena screeched and fell onto Justin's body as her mother and grandmother tried to pull her away. Dr. Nettles guided her from the room when she wouldn't stop crying.

Gramma Grace drove them back to get Dr. Nettles car and headed to the funeral parlor to make arrangements for Arnold's funeral.

"I don't even know Justin's parents' address or phone number. What do I do?"

"Don't worry, honey. The police will take care of that. I will get the number from them and then you can speak with them. It will be a difficult conversation but I think they would appreciate hearing from you."

"But they don't even know me."

"They will soon."

Athena did finally reach Justin's parents and they cried together over his loss. They had his body moved to his hometown and buried next to his grandparents. Athena flew to Ohio to attend the funeral which was held after her father's. She left right afterward feeling like she didn't belong. How could she? They would never forgive her for what had happened to their son.

CHAPTER TWENTY-ONE

A Week later

"How are you feeling, Athena?"

"I'm doing better but…"

"But what?" Dr. Jasper asked as he patiently waited for her to respond.

"I don't want to take any medication. I'm sleeping better now without anything. My dreams have stopped."

"I'm happy to hear that. But you know you can take the meds I gave you if you can't sleep. You've been through a deep trauma."

"It feels like I am living the nightmare with what happened."

"I understand. How is your mother doing? Is she staying with you?"

"Yes, we are still staying at the beach house that belongs to Dr. Nettles. My grandmother is there too. She's worried and is keeping her eye on us."

"That's good. She sounds like a caring person."

"Yes, she's the best. I wouldn't have had a happy childhood without her. My father was…"

"I know it's difficult to talk about him now but take your time."

"I don't want to talk about him. I'm angry about what he did. I may never forgive him."

"That is understandable."

"He took away someone who I cared for and with whom I could possibly have had a future."

"It was a terrible accident, Athena. I'm sure he didn't intend to kill Justin and himself."

"But, I saw this happen before in a nightmare. It was meant to happen eventually."

"You saw it in a dream? When was this? You didn't mention it before."

"I know. I was afraid that you would think that I was crazy."

"No, not at all, Athena. I know your family history of being clairvoyant. Dr. Nettles told me about your grandmother and her psychic abilities."

"He did? I wasn't aware that he even knew about my grandmother and what she is capable of seeing."

"I guess he knows more about your family than you imagined. In fact, he wants to see you after our appointment is over. He's worried about you. I am to call him when we're finished here."

"I'm fine. I'm more worried about my mother. She has been so quiet lately. She hasn't said a thing since this happened. I think she blames herself for my father's death. I don't understand why though."

"Has your mother told you that?"

"Not really but her actions show how she feels. My grandmother told me to let her grieve in peace. She'll come to terms about my father's death eventually."

"I see."

"Why do you do that?"

"What?"

"Why do you say, I see, if you really don't?"

"I'm sorry I didn't realize I did that."

Athena couldn't help but feel badly when she saw the doctor's shocked reaction.

"I'm sorry. I didn't mean to hurt you in any way."

"No problem, Athena. It takes a lot more than that to rile me."

"That's good to know. So, are we finished?"

"Are you in a hurry to go somewhere?"

"No, but aren't you supposed to call Dr. Nettles now?"

"Athena, I think it's time for you to go to another doctor. I don't think I can help you anymore."

"What? Was it something I said? I'm sorry if it was." Athena folded her hands in her lap and looked dejected.

Dr. Jasper smiled and handed her a slip of paper. "Here is the name of a reputable doctor. I will send over your records to her."

"I don't understand, Dr. Jasper."

"Well, let me know when you have made your first appointment and I will share my reasons with you. Now, I'll call Dr. Nettles. He's waiting outside my office."

Athena stared at Dr. Jasper and shook her head. She was thoroughly confused. What was that all about?

Dr. Nettles knocked on the door and came in with a smile on his pleasant face.

"Athena, it's so good to see you. How have you been feeling?"

"I'm well, thank you, Dr. Nettles. How are you?"

"Fine, Athena. I've been worried about you and your mother. Please feel free to stay at the beach house for as long as you want. You can call me anytime you need anything. I will be by to check up on you both in a couple of days. Okay?"

"Okay. We can't thank you enough for all you have done for us. Mom didn't want to go back to the house. She can't go there. I guess the memories of Dad are there. I can understand that. I don't want to go back there either."

"I'm sorry about what happened, Athena. It must be difficult for you to lose both your father and your boyfriend."

"Yes, to one and no to the other. I disliked my father for what he did to my mother all those years. I can't forgive him even now that he is gone. As for Justin, I cared for him. We were just getting to know one another. It was…"

Dr. Nettles patted Athena's hand and placed a box of tissues in front of her.

"It's all right, Athena. I understand. You are still in shock over the loss. Even though you didn't think you loved your father, you did care for him because he was your father. It was a difficult relationship. I'm sorry about that. It was a horrible accident. You and your mother need time to get over this. I am here if either of you need me. Dr. Jasper is too."

He exchanged puzzled looks with Dr. Jasper after Dr. Jasper shook his head.

"Well, I'll need to finish up my rounds. Remember, I am only a phone call away, Athena."

"Thank you, Dr. Nettles. See you soon."

"Yes, you will. Take care, dear."

Dr. Jasper stopped Dr. Nettles and whispered in his ear, "I need to talk to you outside."

Dr. Nettles nodded and smiled at Athena as he turned to leave.

"Well, I guess we are all done here too, Dr. Jasper. Thanks for the last visit. I will call this other doctor soon," Athena announced in a sad voice.

"Athena, please remember to call me after you make an appointment. Okay? There is something I need to tell you."

"Okay." Athena didn't meet Dr. Jasper's eyes and left his office feeling dejected.

Dr. Jasper followed Athena out and met Dr. Nettles in the hall. They waited until Athena had left the building before talking.

"What was that about, Nick?"

"I'm sorry about being so evasive. I had to break off with Athena as her doctor. I gave her the number of a respected colleague of mine to do follow up."

"What? Why did you do that? Is she not happy with you?"

"Oh no, not at all. I think she feels comfortable with me. It's just me. I have feelings for her and I can't continue to be her doctor if I feel this way. It's not ethical. I want to ask her out for a date."

"Oh, I see." Dr. Nettles smiled.

"Don't let Athena hear you say that!" Dr. Jasper chuckled.

"What?"

"Never mind. So, what do you think about my dating her?"

"I think that's an excellent idea. She needs someone in her life. She lost two men who she cared for. Even if she doesn't think she loved her father, I think she did. She is angry with him and in shock."

"Yes, I agree. I feel I can help her more if I get closer to her. I want to get to know her better too. I asked her to call me as soon as she made an appointment with the other doctor. I promised to explain my reasons for transferring her elsewhere. I know she is feeling dejected about me dumping her onto another psychiatrist. I hope she will forgive me."

"I think she will once you explain your reasoning to her."

"I hope so."

Dr. Nettles shook hands with Dr. Jasper and wished him good luck and went on his way to continue rounds.

What Dr. Jasper didn't see, was the wide smile on Dr. Nettles face as he nearly skipped his way down the corridor. Things were working out as he had hoped when he had first asked Dr. Jasper to see Athena.

***

Athena got into her car and sat there. She could feel the tears burning her eyes. What was that all about? Dr. Jasper didn't want to see her anymore?

What did she do? Doesn't he like her? She thought, we clicked when we had lunch together after he picked her up from the hospital. It was a special time. She remembered feeling guilty about it because of Justin, but now Justin is…" Athena covered her face in her hands and cried. Her shoulders trembled and she wept until she couldn't produce any more tears.

She sat back and sighed heavily. Now what? She guessed she would have to call that doctor. What was her name? She looked at the paper Dr. Jasper had given her – Dr. Carrie Harris.

She called her and explained that she was being referred by Dr. Jasper. She made an appointment for the following week and learned that Dr. Harris' office was in the same building as Dr. Jasper's.

She started her car and drove home. She wanted to pick up some clothes and grab a couple of bottles of wine. She could definitely use a drink. Also, she had planned to surprise her mother and grandmother with lunch. She would stop off at her favorite sub place and pick up some meatball and chicken cutlet subs to bring back to the beach house.

She pressed her mother's number and waited.

"Hi honey. How did your appointment go?"

"Fine, Mom. Listen I need to go home first and pick up some more clothes. I will bring lunch back with me, Okay? Is there anything else you or Gramma need?"

"Well, we could use a bottle of wine. You need more clothes? You already brought a ton with you."

"I know but I need a few more things. About the wine, I'm ahead of you there. I planned on grabbing a couple more bottles from my stash at home. Be there in an hour or so."

"Okay. Thanks, honey. See you then."

Before she hung up she asked, "Are you feeling better, Mom?"

"Yes, Athena. I had a nice nap and your grandmother and I are playing cards. Of course, not her tarot cards."

"Well, that's good. See you soon. Love you, Mom."

"Love you too, sweetheart."

CHAPTER TWENTY-TWO

Even though she had already brought many outfits to the beach Athena picked out a few more outfits, a jacket, sweater and sweatshirt and threw them into a shopping bag. She added three bottles of wine to the bag and headed out the door. Next stop was the sub shop.

As she drove along in a stupor, her phone rang. She looked at the screen and noticed it was her best friend, Fran.

"Hey, Fran. How are you? I was thinking of calling you later."

"I'm fine but how are you? I wanted to call you sooner but I knew that you were busy with your father's funeral. We didn't get to talk for long at the wake and funeral. I wanted to give you some time. I'm so sorry about Justin. I can't believe that happened like in your dream!"

"I know. It was a shock to me too. I was hoping that it was only a dream and that it wouldn't mean anything. I'm doing okay, really. I have been worried about my mother. But I just talked to her after my appointment with Dr. Jasper and she sounds better."

"Oh, that's a relief. I was worried about her too. She was clearly in shock at the funeral. She barely said anything. I tried to talk to her but there was no response. I hope she doesn't feel responsible for your father's death."

"No, I don't think so. At least, I hope she doesn't. She has been harboring so much hatred and anger against him. So have I."

"Well, of course. You both have suffered under his rule. He was not an easy man to care for or love."

"Yes, that's true. I saw Dr. Nettles and Dr. Jasper today. Something happened at my appointment with Dr. Jasper that I wanted to share with you."

"What happened? Are you okay?"

"Oh, I'm okay. Nothing to do with my health. It's Dr. Jasper. He released me to the care of another doctor."

"He what? Are you all better?"

"Well, he says that he will explain later after I make my first appointment with the other doctor, which I just did."

"Well, then call him now and find out what he wants to tell you."

"Yeah, I guess I should. He has piqued my curiosity. But I am also feeling dejected for being rejected so to speak."

"Well, call him right now and call me back. I am dying to hear what he has to say for himself."

Athena chuckled at her friend's reaction and said goodbye and called Dr. Jasper. She took a deep breath and waited.

His secretary answered and said, "Hold on one minute, Athena. I will transfer you to his office."

"Thank you."

"Athena, I didn't expect to hear from you so soon. Did you make your appointment with Dr. Harris?"

"Yes."

"Hmm, okay. I guess it's my turn to explain my actions to you. First, let me say that it has been a pleasure to treat you. I didn't do this because I think you are all better. On the contrary, you need to continue with a psychiatrist until you feel well enough to stop. I didn't want that doctor to be me because I want to ask you out on a date. This time it will be a real date."

Athena was silent and couldn't get her voice. She never expected this.

"Athena, are you still there?"

"Yes…I'm here. I don't know what to say. I wasn't expecting this."

"Does that mean that you don't want to go out with me?"

"No. I mean yes, I want to go out with you. But I didn't know that you were interested in me that way."

"I felt a connection to you the day we went for lunch. I was hoping you felt something too."

"Well yes, I did. I was going out with Justin at the time but now…"

"I understand. You weren't available then. Are you ready to go out with me this weekend? I don't want to rush you. I know you just lost your boyfriend. But as your former doctor I would recommend that you give me a chance and get to know me outside of the office. If you are not ready, I will understand. I can wait until you are."

"No, I mean. Yes, I'm ready. I will give you a chance," Athena sighed with a smile that he could not see.

"I am so relieved. I was afraid that you would be angry with me for transferring you to another doctor and not want to talk to me ever again."

"Well, I was thinking that, actually. I felt like you dumped me."

"Ha ha, dumped you? That is a strange way to say I released you to another doctor."

"That is what it felt like, Dr. Jasper."

"Now, let's get that corrected."

"What?"

"My name is Nick."

"Okay, Nick. Nice to meet you."

"All right, we got that straight. What time should I pick you up this weekend? How about 7:30 pm? Do you like Asian food, Thai, or Italian or maybe seafood?"

"All of the above. Your choice. I like to be surprised."

"Okay, I will surprise you. See you at 7:30 pm Saturday."

"Sounds good, doctor, err, I mean Nick."

"That's better. I like the way you say my name, Athena. Look forward to seeing you on Saturday."

"Me too. See you then."

Athena ended the call and pulled into the sub shop as she shook her head in disbelief. Who would have thought? A date with Dr. Jasper, or Nick.

She walked on a cloud as she stood in line for the subs. She ordered and paid and left not remembering doing all that.

Once in her car she called Fran and told her about her date.

"I can't believe it! Your doctor asked you for a date? Is he good looking?" Fran couldn't contain her excitement or disbelief.

"Yes and yes! He is very good looking, smart, kind, sweet and thoughtful."

"All that rolled into one package? Wow, you lucked out, girlfriend. That's wonderful! I want all the details on Saturday night or the next day if the date goes over."

"Fran! I don't plan on it being an overnighter. For goodness sakes, girl! What do you think I am?"

"Hmm, let me think about that."

"Hey, stop it right now. We are just getting to know each other outside his practice."

"Okay, time will tell. Well, talk to you later, Athena. Have a great time!"

"Thanks. I'm sure we will."

"Where are you headed now?"

"I'm going back to the beach house with lunch for my mother and grandmother. I need to keep an eye on my Mom. She's having a difficult time."

"She'll be fine. She is free now from fear and abuse."

"Yes, for that I'm thankful. Well, got to go. Talk to you soon, Fran."

"Okay. Love you, Athena."

"Love you back."

Athena drove the rest of the way to the beach house with thoughts of Nick swimming around in her head. She kept seeing his handsome face smiling with gorgeous white teeth, thick dark hair that she wanted to run her fingers through and his great body.

She felt her cheeks flush with heat as her thoughts turned more sexual. She wondered what he looked like without a shirt or pants.

Whoa, she had to slow down. She realized her foot has pressed the gas a little too much with her naughty thoughts. She suddenly felt guilty feeling this way with Justin gone so recently.

She finally pulled into the driveway of the house and grabbed her bags and ran up to the front door. Her mother was waiting for her and opened it abruptly pulling her in.

"What did you do that for, Mom? Are you hungry or maybe a bit thirsty or something?"

"Yes, dear. We're starving and thought you'd never get here. What took you so long?" She took the bags out of Athena's hands and brought them to the kitchen.

"Hello, Athena. How are you dear? You have some color in your cheeks. Looks good on you," Gramma Grace said as she grinned and winked at her.

Athena touched her cheeks, which still felt warm. She smiled at her grandmother and went to find her mother in the kitchen who was laying out the subs on plates and placing filled wine glasses next to each plate.

She went to her bedroom and dropped off her clothes and returned to the kitchen. Her mother and grandmother were already eating and drinking.

They were both in a good mood which made Athena feel better about her mother and less anxious. Maybe her mother was getting over the loss of her father after all.

Athena sat next to them and dug into her sub. She lifted her glass to her mother and grandmother and made a toast. Here's to us, a fresh beginning without any anxiety or stress."

"Here, here," Gramma Grace and Carla said in unison and clinked glasses.

"Mom, what are you going to do with the house?"

"I called a realtor already. It's going on the market but I have to get over there sometime before she does an open house. Can you come with me and help me clean it out?"

"Of course, Mom. I think it will be cathartic for us to clear everything out. It will be like starting all over again. Right?"

"Yes, I guess it will feel like that." Her face took on a sad expression as she was in deep thought over all that had happened.

"It's okay, Carla. I will come over to help you both. I don't want either one of you getting maudlin on me. Let's make this a fun thing. We can throw away all Arnold's things."

"Yes, I think I might enjoy that just a little," Carla chuckled then stopped abruptly, feeling guilty. "I shouldn't be happy about his death. But I can't deny that I am relieved that he is not here to …"

"Of course, dear. We know how you feel. Right, Athena?"

"Yes, we do. I feel that way too, Mom. It's as if a heavy weight has been lifted off of my chest which was threatening to smother me."

"Well said, sweetheart," Gramma Grace said with a smile. "You both deserve to be happy for a change. He was a troubled man and needed help. It's a shame he never went to a psychiatrist. Maybe that would have helped him get over some things."

Carla exchanged wary looks with her mother and interrupted before she could say any more. "Yes, I think you are right, Mother. He definitely needed help. But let's enjoy the rest of our lunch and talk about more pleasant things."

Athena sat and watched the strange exchange between her mother and grandmother but didn't get a chance to ask what that was all about because her phone rang.

"Hello. Yes, this is Athena. Oh yes, I am still interested in the job. Thank you. Thank you so much, Mr. Forester. Okay, Monday will be perfect at 9:00 am. Yes, I look forward to starting too. Thank you again. See you on Monday. Goodbye."

Carla observed her daughter as she spoke and silently clapped hands with her mother in celebration.

"Well, sounds like you got the job, Athena."

"Yes, I did, Mom. I am so excited. This is the first real job and hopefully a permanent one for a long time. I guess things are looking up for me finally."

"Of course they are, sweetheart. You deserve all the happiness in the world. I'm sorry all this happened. Now is the beginning of a new life for you."

"Thanks, Mom. I feel like it is the beginning. This is what I always wanted. I will finally be a journalist."

"We are so proud of you, Athena. This is wonderful! We need to open up a new bottle of wine and celebrate," her grandmother announced as she opened up more wine.

They finally had something to celebrate. But soon there would be some shocking news for Athena that she may or may not want to celebrate.

CHAPTER TWENTY-THREE

Athena felt sleepy after three or more glasses of wine. The three women spread out on the oversized couches and were slowly falling asleep, when Athena's phone rang once again.

Athena answered groggily, "Hello."

"Athena? This is Lucas Strait from Forester Daily."

"Hi Lucas. How are you?"

"Are you all right? You sound a little funny, Athena."

"I'm just fine."

"I see. Have you been drinking?"

"Just a little," Athena giggled.

"Maybe I should call you tomorrow after you sleep it off. I was just calling to congratulate you on your new job. Gabe told me he hired you. You will have an office next to mine. I'm looking forward to working with you."

"Thank you. Me too."

"Hmm, that's funny."

"What's funny?"

"You still talk in a few words even when you are drunk."

"I'm not drunk."

"I think you are, Athena."

"Maybe a little," she hiccupped and laughed.

"Well, I guess if I ask you out for dinner you probably won't remember I did. But let me try. Would you like to go out to dinner on Saturday?"

"I'm busy."

"You're busy. Do you have another date?"

"Yes."

"I see."

Athena chuckled again.

"What's so funny?"

"You."

"Me? What did I say?"

"I see."

"What?"

"Yes."

"Yes what?"

"I see."

"What do you see?"

"Exactly."

"Oh boy, I am really confused. I better let you sleep it off and call you tomorrow. Sleep well, Athena."

"You too. Night."

Athena laid down on the couch and grabbed a throw pillow and fell promptly asleep. Her mother and grandmother were already sleeping.

***

A couple hours later, Carla woke up and went into the kitchen for a drink of water. She looked at the clock and realized that she had been sleeping for a couple of hours. Her mother and daughter were still sleeping on the couches.

She picked up her cell and called Dr. Nettles. She went into her bedroom and sat down on the bed and waited for him to answer. She felt it was time to tell him what she had been keeping from him for too long.

"Hello, Dr. Nettles speaking."

"Dr. Nettles, it's Carla."

"Oh, Carla. How are you? I was going to call you after my last patient."

"I wanted to talk to you. Can you come up to the beach?"

"Of course. Is everything all right?"

"Yes, but I need to tell you something in person."

"Okay. I will be there in an hour or two. Is that all right?"

"Yes, that's fine. We can have dinner together if you like."

"I was just going to offer to bring you all out to dinner."

"No, I think it should be just you and me. This is something that I need to say without the others."

"That sounds ambiguous to me. Are you sure you are all right?"

"Yes, definitely. No worries. This is something that needs to be said."

"It only gets more mysterious. I can't wait to hear what you have to say."

"I hope you will… Never mind. See you later, doctor."

"Yes, I look forward to it. I'll make reservations – seafood or Asian or something else?"

"Your choice. I will eat either."

***

Athena woke up and looked around. "Mom?"

Gramma Grace woke up when she heard Athena's voice. "What's wrong, Athena?"

"I was looking for Mom. She's not here."

Carla walked out to the living room when she heard Athena's voice. "I'm right here, dear. I was in my bedroom. What's the matter?"

"I was worried when I woke up and didn't see you here."

"That is how you were when you were just a child. You would get anxious if you didn't see me nearby."

"I did? Well, I guess I still need you close by, Mom." Athena got up from the couch and hugged her mother.

That's just what I needed. A tight hug from my little girl." She hugged Athena back and chuckled.

"Except, Mom, I am all grown up."

"Yes, you are. And, such a beautiful young woman you have become. Sit down next to me, honey. There is something I need to tell you."

Gramma Grace smiled and nodded at Carla. "Yes, it is about time she knows, Carla."

"What is this all about?" Athena frowned and rubbed her temples in preparation.

"This is something that I should have shared with you and your father a long time ago. I had a feeling about this and didn't realize until you were older and in high school when you had a blood test."

"What are you talking about, Mom?"

"Carla, get on with it. Just tell her. You are being so cryptic. How is she supposed to know what you are talking about?"

"I know, I know. Okay, I'll spit it out. Dr. Nettles is your father."

Athena felt like she had been slapped in the face. She was so shocked and her face blanched as she felt tears burning her eyes.

"What?"

"I know it's hard to believe but it's true. I should try to explain a little more. I'm sorry for shocking you, honey. It happened just once. It was over a year after your sister died. I was still depressed and distraught and called Dr. Nettles. He came right over to check on me. I was emotional and couldn't stop crying over losing Alyssa. He held me tightly and the next minute he was kissing me and… It shouldn't have happened. I know, but I needed someone to hold me and your father wouldn't even look at me after her death. He blamed me."

"I'm shocked, Mom. But not for what you did. It's okay. I understand. You needed someone and Dad wasn't there for you. But I'm surprised you didn't tell me all these years. Did Dad know?"

"I didn't know right away either until you were in high school and had a blood test. Your blood type didn't match either one of ours. I did sleep with your father a little while later after Dr. Nettles, so I didn't even think about that when I learned I was pregnant a few months later. I think he did suspect after you were born that you weren't his. But he never asked me though. Of course, I didn't want to tell him about the possibility that you could be Dr. Nettles or couldn't until I realized the truth many years later. I was afraid of what he would do to me and you if he knew."

"I understand. I'm sure he would have wanted to kill us both. Does Dr. Nettles know I am his daughter?"

"No. I plan on telling him tonight. He is coming up and taking me out to dinner. He offered to take all of us, but I thought it would be better if I told him alone like I did with you."

"That's fine, Mom. He needs to hear this from you alone. I think he will be as shocked as I was. He may need to come to terms with it. Do you think he will be happy to have me as a daughter?"

"I'm sure he will be ecstatic. Who wouldn't want a beautiful daughter like you? He will be thrilled but I'm sure quite surprised at the same time."

"Do you have feelings for Dr. Nettles, Mom?"

"Well, I…don't know. I admire and respect him and like him for all he has done for us. But love takes time. Maybe time will tell if this is love."

"Sounds like you love him, Mom. He is a wonderful man, kind, caring and sensitive. Who wouldn't love him? I have always loved him as a friend. Now I can love him as a father."

"That's wonderful, honey. Thank you. I needed to hear that. Yes, he is a wonderful man. Maybe I do love him more than I ever imagined. It's been a hard life with your father. I didn't know what love was, only fear, anger and hurt. Dr. Nettles was always there for me in tough times."

"Oh Mom, I'm so sorry for all the fear, anger and hurt you had to endure. I was not aware of it all. I don't know how I missed it. I guess I didn't want to believe that my father could do what he did to you. I am relieved that he isn't my father now. I was fearful of carrying his genes. I didn't want to be like him."

"You could never have been like him even if you did carry his genes. You are sweet, loving, caring and sensitive just like your real father. Thank God for that."

"What time is Dr. Nettles, err I mean, Dad coming to pick you up?"

"Sounds funny, huh?"

"Yes, it feels odd but I'll get used to it."

"He will be here in an hour or so now. I better get ready."

"Where are you going?"

"Don't know. I left it up to him. He said either Asian or seafood." Carla left the room to get ready.

"They are both delicious!"

"Yes, I agree, Athena," Gramma Grace said. "Let's go out too. Once we know where they are going we can go elsewhere."

"Great! I'm starved, Gramma."

"That's my girl, always ready to eat," Gramma Grace chuckled.

They sat around waiting for Dr. Nettles to arrive. All were dressed and ready to go out even if they were going in different directions.

The doorbell rang and everyone jumped. Carla walked quickly to the door and opened it with a wide smile.

"Carla, you look lovely!"

"Thank you, Dr. Nettles. Come in."

"Hello ladies. You both look lovely too. Are you coming with us?"

"No, they are going out somewhere else. Where are you taking me?"

"Well, I know you love both seafood and Asian so I found a place that has both. It's called, The Asian Bistro."

"Hmm, sounds intriguing. Do you want to go now or do you want a drink first?"

"No, let's go. I will buy a bottle of wine for us at the restaurant. Okay?"

"Fine with me. We both may need it."

"What?"

"Never mind. See you later, Athena and Mom." Carla rushed the doctor out the door. She was anxious about what he was going to say after she told him the news.

"What's your hurry, Carla? Are you sure you are all right?"

"Yes, I'm fine. I want to get to the restaurant and discuss something important with you."

"Okay, let's go." The doctor guided Carla to his car and opened the door. He kept his eyes on her as he started the car. She was looking extremely anxious but lovelier than ever. He was thinking about what she had said about this news. He was feeling as anxious as she was about now.

He drove in silence. Both of them were absorbed in their own thoughts.

When they arrived at the restaurant, he got out of the car quickly and opened her door. He reached his hand out to help her out of the car and guided her to the door of the restaurant.

The smells were enticing as they entered the restaurant that had a Koi pond in the middle of the room. A large gong was situated to the right of the door. Lovely colorful Asian prints were scattered around the room and cozy tables and booths were arranged far enough apart to give each party some privacy.

Carla took in her surroundings and began to relax. Everything was going to be okay. They were seated and a bottle of wine was chosen and poured. She took a sip and sat back and smiled at the man who was the father of her daughter. She wondered what he would say when she told him. She kept her fingers crossed that he would be happy and proud. What was she going to do if he wasn't?

CHAPTER TWENTY-FOUR

Dr. Nettles looked at Carla who was sipping her wine and smiling at him. He had loved this woman for as long as he could remember since the first time he set eyes on her. What could she possibly want to tell him after all these years?

Carla cleared her voice and began, "I guess you must be wondering what I am going to tell you?"

"Yes. I had a difficult time concentrating on my rounds. Thankfully I only had a couple of patients who were being discharged and therefore no problems."

"That's good. I wouldn't want to disrupt you in any way. Your job is too important."

"Yes, it's important but not as important as you are to me, Carla. You know how I feel about you, how I have always felt about you."

"Wait, I am the one who has something to tell you. Please, let me continue." Carla's face reddened as she tried to gather her wits after what he had just announced.

"I need to tell you something that may or may not make you happy. A long time ago you and I were intimate."

"Yes, I remember it clearly."

"Okay, please let me continue, Doctor."

"First, please do not call me 'doctor.' Call me by my first name Ashton or Ash. It's about time you did."

"All right. Ash, please let me continue. Nine months later I had Athena."

"Yes, I remember. She was a beautiful baby. She is even more beautiful as a woman just like her mother."

"Ash, did you hear me? Nine months later I had a baby. You are her father for goodness sakes!"

"Oh, I...I'm Athena's father? Are you sure?"

"Yes, I am. Athena had to have a blood test when she was in high school. I knew my blood type and her fathers but she did not match either of us. Do you remember I asked you what type of blood you had and you told me AB positive? Well, that is what Athena's blood type is. She is yours."

"Oh my goodness. I never suspected that. I remember you asked me that question and it didn't make any sense to me at that time. Now it does though."

"Are you shocked?"

"Well, surprised and a whole lot thrilled to have a daughter. I am over the moon, Carla. I really am. This is not what I expected to hear from you. I thought that you were going to tell me that you didn't want to see me anymore."

"Why would I say that?"

"I don't know."

"Do you care for me at all, Carla?"

"Well, I…admire you and …I am grateful for all the things you have done for me and Athena. You kept me sane in the toughest of times. You were always there for us. You…you were more my husband than Arnold was. You were there for me. I…I do love you, Ash. I guess I always have."

"Oh thank God for that. I am blessed to have you both. I am the happiest man alive right now. I need a drink. How about you? I was wondering what I was going to do without you in my life and now I have both of you. How lucky can a man get?"

"I'm relieved too, Ash. I was worried that you wouldn't want to have a daughter or that you would be upset with me for not telling you all these years."

"No, I'm not upset. How could I ever be upset with you, my love? I know it is too soon but I want you to marry me when you are ready."

"What? Marry you? You want to marry me?"

"Yes. It's something I wanted for a long time but I know that you wouldn't have asked Arnold for a divorce. He wouldn't have let you go anyway."

"That's true. I couldn't get out of that marriage no matter what I did. He wouldn't have released me."

"I don't know what to say, Ash. I am happy for the first time in my life. I feel free without any fear. You make me feel like a new woman. I will give you my answer after a decent time has passed. I am a widow after all."

"Yes, I understand, Carla," Ash chuckled.

"I will be here when you are ready. Now, let's order our food. I am starving!"

"So am I! I could eat a whole Pu Pu platter!" Carla giggled like a school girl.

The meal was exquisite and the wine was delicious. They opened their second bottle and sat back and sighed happily. They couldn't take their eyes off of one another like two lovesick kids.

"I love you, Carla. I can't wait to be your husband. But for now I look forward to making up for lost time with my daughter. Let's go back home. The beach house can be your home from now on. You can sell your house and move in permanently."

"Okay, but I'm not ready to live together. I need to have some time alone. My house is going on the market soon. Once it's sold I will move in but you need to give me time."

"I will give you all the time you need, Carla. I have waited this long. I can wait a little longer."

"Thank you, Ash. Now I'm ready to go home. Thank you for the delicious meal. It was wonderful."

"You are welcome. It was wonderful!" Ash beamed and took Carla's hand in his and squeezed it.

Once they got into the car Ash turned to her, "Does Athena know about me?"

"Yes, she does." Carla smiled with tears in her eyes.

"Why are you crying, dear?"

"I'm not crying. I am just happy and emotional right now. I feel happier than I ever remember feeling for a long, long time."

"Me too, my love." Ash lifted her hand and brought it to his lips.

CHAPTER TWENTY-FIVE

Ash drove back to the beach but didn't remember doing that. He was absorbed in his thoughts about being a father for the first time. He was finally going to have a family of his own.

He pulled into the driveway and opened the door and took Carla into his arms for a quick hug. They walked up to the door arm in arm and smiled like Cheshire cats.

Peering out of the front windows were Athena and Gramma Grace who had come back from dinner several minutes before. They jumped up and down at the sight of the two love birds heading toward the front door.

Athena pulled open the door as her mother and her father stepped forward ready to open it themselves. She stood in front of them and smiled broadly. Before she could give her father a hug, he pulled her into his arms and held onto her as if she would try to get away.

Athena responded in kind, while tears filled her eyes. She choked up when she tried to speak. She stepped back but gripped Ash's hands and squeezed them.

He nodded and smiled and said, "I feel the same way, Athena, speechless. But I want you to know that I have always loved you like a daughter and now you are mine to love even more. I am the happiest father in the whole world."

"Thank you, Dad. I have loved you too! You were the father that I never had. You were always there for me. You were the one to listen to me, hold me when I cried and told me that everything was going to be all right."

Ash hugged her again as tears brimmed in his eyes. He looked over at Carla who was already crying and being hugged by her mother.

"Wait a minute," he said. "This looks like a funeral instead of a happy time. Enough with the tears. Let's have a drink. I can make a delicious sangria. It's world famous. Who's up for one?"

Hands were raised all around as they sat at the counter and watched Ash prepare his famous sangrias.

The night passed quickly as they sat around and talked and laughed. They were feeling and looking like a family.

Carla popped some corn and passed it around when she started to feel the sangria going to her head. She felt as if she would burst with how happy she was feeling. Is this how it feels to have a good life and love the man who was to be her husband? She realized that she never felt this way about Arnold. She put thoughts of him away as she sat next to her daughter and Ash who were deep in conversation and laughing so hard they were crying.

It was wonderful to see her daughter so happy too. Carla looked over at her mother who appeared to be somewhere else. She wore a concerned frown on her face.

Gramma Grace observed her daughter and granddaughter and was thrilled that they were both finally going to have a happy life free of fear, anger and hurt. She looked up at Carla and their eyes met. What Grace had seen in her mind she could not share right now. She didn't want to spoil the festive feeling in the air with unhappy news of future things to come. She often wished she didn't have this power to see into the future at times like this.

Ash looked at his watch and realized it was quite late. He stood up and hugged both of his girls and gave Gramma Grace a quick hug too, much to her surprise.

"I hope I didn't overstep my bounds, Grace. But after all, you will be my mother-in-law one day."

"What?" Gramma Grace's eyes opened wide and she looked at her daughter in surprise.

"Yes, Mother. Ash has asked me to marry him. But, I told him that it was too soon after Arnold's death. I need to have some time to gather my thoughts, sell the house and move here."

"You are getting married and moving here, Mom? That's wonderful!"

"Yes, but we won't be living together until we get married. I don't want to rush things."

Grace interjected, "Oh of course not, dear. You have waited thirty years why not wait a little longer. Are you crazy? You deserve to have a good life and be happy. Why wait? Life is too short, Carla."

"I like the way you think, Grace. I feel that way too. We have waited long enough. But I want Carla to have some time to collect herself. I don't want to rush her. I have waited all my life for her, a few months more won't matter. We will be together daily at least that is what I plan to do." He turned to Carla and smiled and winked.

"I plan on calling you every day and coming up here every weekend and taking you out to wine and dine properly. I don't want to waste a minute of the time we have together."

"Yes, I agree, Mom. You and Dad should be together. Don't wait. Gramma and I can plan the wedding. It will be a simple affair. It will only be the four of us after all. Gramma and I will be your bridesmaids and witnesses."

"We could have it right on the beach in front of the house and around the pool area. I will take the photos at no charge," Grace added.

"I will write up the announcement in the paper and do all the decorating in the house. We can order the food in from a local restaurant," Athena couldn't contain her excitement as her voice rose on every word.

Carla shook her head, "You both have everything under control. I can see that. But what say do we, the ones who are going to get married, have?"

"Umm, well, you can decide what you want to eat."

"Wow, thanks," Carla chuckled.

Ash joined in and said, "All sounds good to me. When should we do all this?"

"I will let you know, Ash. It's getting late. I think we should call this a night. You must have patients early and rounds to make."

"Yes and yes, but first I need to give my intended a hug and kiss. Please excuse me, ladies, while I give my lovely bride-to-be a proper goodnight."

Gramma Grace and Athena left the room and threw kisses to the happy couple. They went to their bedrooms and got ready for bed. Athena called out to her grandmother, "Gramma, come in here when you are changed."

"Okay. Be right there, sweetheart."

As they both sat on the edge of Athena's bed, they talked about what had transpired. So much had happened in the past several hours.

"I am over the moon, Gramma. I can't believe that Dr. Nettles is my father. I am so relieved and thrilled that I have such a wonderful man for a father and soon he will be married to Mom."

"Yes, he is a special man. I am happy for you both. Take each day as it comes, honey. Don't rush your mother. She needs time to adjust and take care of things with the house. She has to put things in order before she begins a new life with Ash."

"I know, but I can't believe all this. It's incredible. I'm shocked that Mom could keep this from me for so many years. I'm also glad that Dad or Arnold didn't know about this. Come to think of it, he did say something to me when I talked to him about taking me in place of Justin. He said, "Why would I want you. You aren't even my..." He never finished his sentenced. Do you think he meant to say that I am not even his daughter?"

"Possibly. I guess. But don't worry about it now, honey. It is all over now. He's gone now.""

"Yes, it is. But...I am still angry with Arnold for taking Justin's life. He was too young and had so many more years before him. He and I may have gotten together in the future. Now..."

"Athena, please don't be upset. It was an accident. Your father didn't plan to die. Thank God that what he planned to do to your mother didn't come to fruition. He would have taken her life. You know that, don't you? He may not have let Justin go either. In a sense, Justin gave his life for your mother's."

"That does sound possible, Gramma Grace. But my nightmares were so confusing. I kept seeing someone else driving and sometimes I was in the car and other times Mom and Dad or Dad and Justin were in the car. I should have told Justin about my dream. Then he would have been more careful around my father."

"We don't know what transpired between them and why he decided to kidnap Justin. How did he even know Justin was your boyfriend? We didn't even know him."

"I think Dad was casing my house for a long time. He must have seen Justin coming and going a few times. In his sick mind, he evidently surmised a way to get to Mom through me."

"Yes, you are right about his sick mind. But let's talk about something more pleasant like when we are going to start preparations for this wedding."

"Wait a minute. You were the one who suggested we give Mom a little time to get acclimated and sell the house."

"Umm yes, I did. But I was hoping that if I suggested something, your mother would do the opposite. She always did when she was younger. She never wanted me to have the last say," Gramma Grace chuckled.

"She did? I didn't know that. Mom always said she was the perfect child. Every time I tested her patience she said she never did that to you."

Gramma Grace choked up laughing and said, "You've got to be kidding? If anyone was perfect, it was you, Athena. You gave her no trouble at all. She was fortunate to have you."

"That's what I kept telling her," Athena joined in the laughter and hugged her grandmother.

They heard Carla coming down the corridor to her room and both of them followed her.

"Hey, what's going on here? Are you two ganging up on me?"

"No, Mom. We want to say congratulations to you for snagging a winner this time."

"Athena! What a thing to say."

"Not really, Carla. She hit it right on the head. He is a winner and you are one lucky lady. Don't let him get away. We are beginning plans for your wedding one month from this weekend."

"What?"

"Yes, Mom. I think that is an excellent idea. Why make poor Dad wait any longer. He loves you and you love him. Tie the knot. I want to be a bridesmaid."

"Let me think about it. I will have to discuss this with Ash too, you know. He is the groom-to-be and has some say in the matter."

"Of course, Mom. Let us know by tomorrow."

"What?"

Athena raced out of her mother's room with her grandmother in tow giggling and conspiring.

"That's the way to handle her, Athena. You must be firm. She takes too long to make a decision. I always told her that since she was a young child. We will take care of everything."

"Yes, we will, Gramma. Now it's time for bed. I think that sangria is going to my head."

"It went to mine a long time ago, dear!" Gramma Grace hugged Athena and went to her room. She had some thinking to do about what was coming.

CHAPTER TWENTY-SIX

The next morning Athena woke up early and made breakfast for her mother and grandmother. It was a time to celebrate the beginning of a new life for all of them.

Gramma Grace and Carla came out to the kitchen once they smelled something delicious cooking.

"What's cooking, Athena? It smells wonderful!" her mother exclaimed as she peeked over her daughter's shoulder.

"It's my special omelets with spinach, mushroom, tomato and feta cheese. I have some raisin toast too, your favorite, Mom."

"Wow, how special. Are we still celebrating?"

"Of course. We are beginning a new happy chapter in our lives. Why not celebrate?"

"Yes, I second that, Athena. Do you need help? I can set the table and dish out some fruit salad to start."

"I'll get the coffee, ladies," Carla announced as she pulled out the ground coffee and pot.

"We have to get Dad to buy some coffee pods and a modern coffee pot."

"I guess. He is a little old fashioned. But, don't worry. I will get him up to speed," Carla chuckled.

"That's my girl," Grace said with a wink.

"So, what are you going to do today, Athena? Do you have a date?"

"Not today but Saturday."

"We can all go down to the beach and take a long walk and make some decisions about the upcoming nuptials."

"Perfect, Gramma. Let's enjoy our breakfast and then we will take that walk. After eating all this we may need it."

"I agree, Athena. You outdid yourself. This is the best omelet I have ever had."

"Thanks, Mom."

The three were cleaning up the kitchen after breakfast, when Athena's phone rang.

"You get that. We'll finish up here, honey," her mother stated as she scooted her daughter aside.

Athena looked at her cell screen and saw a few texts from Lucas and now the call.

"Hello."

"Athena? How are you today? I wanted to ask you again for that date. I called you last night but you were three sheets to the wind, my dear, and in no condition to answer me."

"Oh, I don't remember you calling."

"Well, I want to take you out for lunch today and dinner on Saturday."

"You didn't even ask if I am busy or not."

"Are you?"

"Yes on both days."

"Oh, I see."

"Well, what about right now? Do you want to go out to breakfast or a brunch?"

"No, I already ate and besides, I am busy, Lucas."

"Well, what day or night are you not busy?"

"All of them."

"What?"

"You can't possibly be busy every day and night."

"Why not?"

"No one is that busy."

"I am."

"Oh, we are back to that now, are we?"

"What?"

"You are back to a few words."

"So?"

"Well, I want to see you and won't take no for an answer."

"I've got to go now, Lucas. See you on Monday."

"Wait…"

"What was that about, Athena?" her mother asked.

"Oh, it's a guy I met when I went for my interview at the Forester Daily. He is becoming a pest. He said he called me last night. I don't remember. My mind was foggy after the sangrias and I did take a nap."

"I remember you getting a call last night but didn't ask you who it was. I fell asleep too," Gramma Grace stated with a frown on her brow.

"Oh dear. We don't need another crazy man in your life, Athena. Ignore him," her mother exclaimed with concern.

"He will be right next to me at work. We have offices side by side. I will be working closely with him. I thought he was a nice guy when we first met. I even thought that he...oh, never mind. But now, I don't know."

"That's not good, Athena. I think you should reconsider getting this position," Gramma Grace suggested.

"Why do you say that, Gramma?" Athena looked closely at her grandmother's face that was deep in concentration. "Are you trying to tell me something?"

"Mom, answer her. What is it? Do you see something in the future that is something to be concerned about?" Carla gripped her mother's hands.

"What's wrong, Gramma? Please tell me."

"Nothing, honey. I am concerned about who you go out with. This man doesn't sound like someone who is worthy of you. He sounds too clingy and possessive even before you go out together."

Athena frowned. "Well, we did go out for a coffee and pastry after we met at the office after my interview."

"Oh, I see."

"You too?"

"Me too, what, honey?" her grandmother asked.

"Well, it seems that every man I speak to says that. What do they think they see?"

"I haven't the foggiest," she responded with a smirk.

"Athena, take it slowly with this one. He sounds like he likes you too much and wants to possess you already. Keep your distance if you can."

"I will, Mom. I certainly will do my best at work too."

They grabbed a light jacket since the weather had suddenly turned a little cooler and headed out to the beach for their walk.

***

Lucas was heading over to Athena's house at the same time and was hoping to convince her to go to lunch and/or dinner with him this weekend.

Luckily for Athena, he didn't know she was not at home but at the beach house.

When he arrived at Athena's house, he rang the bell and waited. He kept ringing it a few more times.

Where was she? Is she avoiding me for some reason?

He went back to the office to do some work until he could figure out what to do next.

Mark was sitting at his desk looking disheveled as usual. "Hey, Mark. How are you? Boyfriend problems?"

"Huh? No! I'm fine, Lucas. Aren't you supposed to be in the meeting with the other reporters?"

"What meeting?"

"The one at 10:00 this morning. You are over an hour late. Gabe won't be happy."

"No problem. I have Gabe wrapped right here." Lucas lifted his little finger and waved it at Mark.

Mark mumbled something under his breath at Lucas.

"What did you say?"

"Oh, nothing important. Don't forget the meeting, Lucas."

"Yeah, I'm going. But first, do you have an address for that new girl, Athena?"

"Why?"

"I need to drop something off to her for Gabe."

"Let me see. Yes, there are two addresses she listed, one is in town and the other is at Long Beach."

"Long beach? Can I have that one?"

"Okay." Mark wrote down the address but watched Lucas' face as he smirked and grabbed it out of Mark's hands.

Mark sat back in his chair and sighed. He only hoped that he hadn't done the wrong thing by giving Lucas Athena's address. He pressed Gabe's office line and waited.

"Yah, what do you want, Mark? Do I have another appointment?"

"No, Gabe. I just have a question for you."

"Okay, shoot."

"Did you give Lucas something to take to Athena?"

"What? Something for Athena? What's that?"

"I don't know. Lucas told me that he needed Athena's address so he could take something to her."

"No, I did not give him anything for Athena. Did you give him her address?"

"Yes, I did. Is everything all right?"

"I don't know yet. I better call Athena. He can be a pest sometimes when he likes a girl. He may be too pushy with her. I don't want him turning her off from this job before she even begins. Get me her cell, Mark." Gabe turned to his staff who were sitting listening to him. "I'll be back in a minute."

He left the room to make a call.

CHAPTER TWENTY-SEVEN

"Hello. Mr. Forester? How are you? Is everything all right?"

"Athena. I don't want to alarm you, but Lucas is on his way there to see you. He convinced Mark that he needed your address to deliver something to you from me. That is not correct. I did not give him anything for you."

"Oh, should I be concerned?"

"Yes, I was going to get to that."

Carla interrupted Athena on the phone when the doorbell rang and she announced that there was a visitor for her.

Athena looked up from her call and told Mr. Forester that Lucas was there.

"Athena, please wait before you talk to him."

Her mother invited Lucas in after he introduced himself as Athena's fellow reporter. She smiled at this handsome young man and stepped aside for him to enter. Athena was still on the phone as he came closer to her.

"Hi Athena. I thought you might like to go to lunch with me. I can go over some stuff about the job to get you acclimated before you start."

Her mother looked at Athena with a stern expression. "Athena, you have a visitor. It's not polite to be on the phone. Lucas is here to take you to lunch."

"Okay, Mom. I see him. Let me finish my call."

Athena whispered to her boss, "I need to go. I will talk to you later."

"Athena, don't hang up. I need to tell you 'something important.'"

But she had not heard the 'something important' part and had already hung up.

Gabe looked at his phone and shook his head as he heard the call end. He buzzed Mark. "Give me Athena's address."

"Is everything okay?"

"Not really, Mark. I wish you hadn't given Athena's address to Lucas. This could be trouble."

Mark read off Athena's beach address with a shaky voice. "What are you going to do, Boss?"

"I need to go see Athena. She could be in trouble."

"What? Is Lucas dangerous?"

"Could be. I want to go there to warn her. I hope I'm not too late because he is already there."

"Do you want me to call the police?"

"No, not yet. I will call them if I have any problem with him. I need to convince him to leave her alone."

***

Athena agreed to go out to lunch with Lucas to let him get her up to snuff on her new position, or so he said. She didn't understand why Mr. Forester had called. He sounded concerned."

Lucas escorted Athena to his bright red Mustang and held open the door for her. He smiled showing his pearly whites and got in and drove away.

"Where are we going to lunch, Lucas? There are a few good restaurants around here."

"Yes, I scouted them out on my way here. I thought you might like the Seafood Catch. That's not too far."

"Yes, that sounds good. I've been there already recently with my mother and grandmother. But I'm not really hungry, Lucas."

"Well, that's okay. You can have something light."

"So, what did you want to share with me about the job? Is there something that I need to know before I start?"

"Not really. Gabe will get you up to date on day one. I just wanted to see you again. I thought we had a connection the first time we were together."

"Oh, I see?"

"Back to three words again? I thought it was nice while it lasted that you were talking in a complete sentence."

"Oh,"

"I want to get to know you better, Athena, since we will be working closely together in the office."

"Okay. I guess that's good."

"What's good?"

"To get to know the person with whom I will be working closely."

"Yes, exactly what I said. I want to get to know you much better. I need to know about what you like to eat, what are your favorite things to do, and if you like me."

"Now you are asking me after we arrive at the restaurant what I like to eat?"

"Oh, sorry. Do you like seafood?"

"Yes, I do," Athena chuckled at the shocked expression on Lucas' face.

"Oh, phew, that's good!"

Lucas pulled into a parking space and jumped out and opened the door for Athena. He offered her his arm and escorted her into the restaurant.

Athena smiled at the gallant way he was treating her. Maybe he is a nice guy after all, she thought.

Lunch went smoothly. They shared a lot about themselves, their likes, dislikes and what they like to eat and their hobbies.

"You have answered all my questions, Athena. The only one left is, do you like me?"

"Yes, I do. You may be a little pushy at times like coming up to my address and expecting me to go out to lunch with you."

"Wow, two sentences at once! I am impressed!"

"Ha."

"Back to one word now? I shouldn't have said anything about that."

"What do you want to tell me about the job?"

"Oh nothing in particular except that Gabe wants your reports on time. He decides what goes in the paper, not you."

"I see."

"I'm glad you do. He can be pretty fussy about things but he is a good guy to work for."

"That's good to hear."

"Do you want some more wine?"

"No, I had enough."

"Okay, I had enough too. What about coffee? I don't want this time to end with you. I'm really enjoying getting to know you."

"Yes. That would be perfect."

"Are you having a good time too?"

"Yes. It has been a lovely lunch. The shrimp cocktail was wonderful!"

"That's nice that you feel that way. We will be seeing each other five days a week for eight hours a day. I hope you don't get sick of me."

"That is possible, I guess."

"Really? You think you will get tired of me?"

"Time will tell. Lucas, why did your co-worker leave, the one I am replacing?"

"Oh, she…got another job. I think this position was a starting job for her. She had higher aspirations."

"Oh, I see."

"Would you like dessert too, Athena, to go with the coffee?"

"No thank you. The shrimp cocktail was more than enough for me."

"Okay. I'll get the check."

***

Back at the beach house Gabe had arrived and was sitting with Carla and Grace having a cup of coffee.

"Mr. Forester, why did you rush up here to see Athena?" Grace asked with concern.

"I wanted to discuss something with her about Lucas."

"What about Lucas? He seems to be a nice young man, so polite and considerate. He opened the car door for Athena. I watched from the front window," Carla stressed with a raised brow.

"Oh, yes. He can be that way. But…there are other times when he is not so considerate. I was

328

concerned when my aide told me that he was on his way up here to see Athena."

"What are you concerned over, Mr. Forester?" Grace queried as she put down her coffee and focused on his expressions.

"First, please call me Gabe. I tried to tell Athena on the phone but she hung up before I could tell her about Lucas."

"Please, Gabe. Share your concerns with us. Should we be worried about how he is treating my daughter?"

"Not yet. But maybe later on if she rebuffs his attention."

"He doesn't like women to do that? Is he dangerous?" Grace pushed further.

"I'm sorry. I should explain something first. I don't want you to jump to conclusions. It's just that…"

"What? You must share whatever it is that is making you upset, Gabe. This is my daughter. Please explain," Carla requested adamantly.

"Okay. Well, it was his former co-worker, Sharleen. She worked with Lucas for several years. She kept coming in to see me and complain about him hanging around her desk and not leaving. She said he would say suggestive things to her and asked her out on many occasions. She kept rejecting him."

"And, what happened?"

"She left. She quit her job when he wouldn't leave her alone. It all began innocently but then he couldn't stop. He became an annoyance to her so much that it affected her work. I had to let her go."

"Why didn't you fire Lucas?" Grace asked in confusion.

"I confronted him but he denied any of it. He said she came on to him. I did believe her and I tried to put them farther apart on projects and offices. It didn't work. Lucas is the best reporter I have ever had. I couldn't let him go."

"Do you think that he will do this to Athena?"

"It's possible, if she rejects him like Sharleen did."

"Sounds like he could be a danger to Athena. You have to keep them apart and watch over her," Carla suggested vehemently

"Yes, I plan to do that, Carla. I promise. I will also have a conversation with Lucas with a warning that he will be fired if there are any complaints against him from any more women in the company."

Carla sighed heavily, "Thank you, Gabe. I appreciate that. Athena has been through enough at this time and doesn't need someone like this in her life."

Grace sat back and nodded to Carla and Gabe but was silent. She was working out something in her head and was not ready to share it.

As this conversation was going on Lucas drove up with Athena and parked his flashy Mustang and escorted her to the door.

Athena took out her key and was about to open the door when Lucas turned her toward him.

"What are you doing, Lucas?"

"I wanted to kiss you. Don't I deserve at least a little kiss after the wonderful lunch I provided?"

"I did say thank you already. Let me go."

"Okay, I'm sorry for being pushy. Can I see you again?"

"Not right now. I will see you next week at work."

"Okay fine, Athena. But, can I at least come in for a little while?"

"No. Goodbye, Lucas."

"Goodbye then, Athena." He stomped off in a huff and slammed his door and gunned the engine as he drove away.

Athena watched him leave and shook her head.

When she went into the house, she saw her mother, grandmother and her new boss in deep discussion.

"Mr. Forester? What are you doing here?"

Gabe jumped up nearly spilling his coffee. "Athena, are you all right? Where's Lucas?"

"He left. I didn't invite him in which didn't make him too happy. Why are you here? And, why the questions about Lucas?"

"When I found out from Mark that Lucas was coming here, I was concerned. He can be a little pushy at times."

"Yes, I agree. He can be pushy but not a threat to me in any way."

"Well, that's good to hear." Gabe sat back and relaxed and finished his coffee.

"But I still don't understand why you came all this way just to ask me if I am all right."

"Okay, I better explain. I told your mother and grandmother all about Lucas before you arrived home. It's time I share this with you too, especially since you will be working closely with him."

"This is getting a little weird. What's the problem?"

Gabe sat forward on the couch and stared at Athena with a serious expression. "I don't want to alarm you, Athena, but I feel it's necessary to tell you a little about Lucas."

Athena sat down across from her employer and exchanged nervous glances with her mother and grandmother before focusing on Gabe again.

"The reason there is an opening at my paper is behind all this mystery. The woman's name was Sharleen. No need to tell you her last name. She worked for me for several years, was a good reporter, always on time with her column and thorough. She was an all-around good employee and a pleasant person."

"I see."

"Yes, I'm sorry, I'll move it along faster. Don't want you to be upset about my timing. Being a newspaper man I tend to tell the whole picture."

"Yes, I can see that."

"Sorry again, Athena. Well, Sharleen came to me one day with a complaint about Lucas. She said he was bothering her while she was trying to work. He kept coming back to her all day long and interrupting her. He would ask her out a dozen times. She couldn't get rid of him and wasn't interested in him in that way."

"Oh, I see."

"This went on for days, weeks, then months and years. I kept changing her around from assignments with other reporters in place of Lucas. But he continued to annoy her. I even changed her office to another floor but you can imagine what I will say next. Yes, he went up to her new office and bothered her there."

"Wait a minute, Mr. Forester. You mean to tell me that you didn't speak to Lucas about all this?"

"Call me Gabe please. Oh, I certainly did speak to him on numerous occasions. You have to understand. Lucas is my best reporter and always gets the scoop on the latest news first before anyone else. I couldn't fire him. I had to let Sharleen go. But she asked to leave before I could do that."

"Oh, I see. Do you think the same thing will happen to me?"

"It probably will. He is already chasing after you for a date, isn't he?"

"Well, I guess he is. We have already gone out for coffee and now lunch. He asked me to go to dinner but I said no."

"I'm sorry to distress you like this before you even begin work, Athena. I will keep close watch over you and put you on different assignments than Lucas. I want you to feel comfortable in your working place. If he ever bothers you to the point of annoyance, please let me know. I will take care of him."

"Thank you, Gabe. I appreciate that but I think maybe I should look for another position. This may not be the right fit for me."

"Oh no, I didn't mean to chase you away. I want you to come work for me. You are perfect for the job."

"No, I don't think I am. If a supervisor handles a situation like you did with Sharleen then I don't want to work for you, Mr. Forester. Thank you for coming here to explain all this. I appreciate the warning."

Carla and Grace sat stunned at what Athena had just said to her new supervisor. They were speechless and got up only after Gabe did and walked him to the door.

Gabe turned and looked at Athena but she didn't meet his eye. "I'm sorry, Athena. If you change your mind please call me. Goodbye."

Turning to Carla and Grace he said, "Thank you for the coffee. Nice to meet you both. I'm sorry for bothering you."

Carla responded, "You're welcome, Gabe. Nice to meet you too. I don't know what to say. My daughter is very strong minded."

"Yes, I can see that. But that is a good thing. I like a strong woman. I wish her all the best. I hope she will change her mind."

Grace smiled and said, "Don't bet on it, Gabe."

CHAPTER TWENTY-EIGHT

Gabe got back to the office in a funk and only told Mark what had happened after he asked repeatedly what was wrong.

Mark responded warily, "I don't want to tell Lucas about this. He won't be happy. He will try to talk Athena into coming."

"No, he won't. I have had enough of him. If he tries to harass her, I will fire him. Then maybe Athena will come work for me," Gabe stated and slammed his office door.

Mark sat back, smiled, and felt calm for once in his life. He whispered under his breath, "It's about time!"

***

Athena got ready for her dinner date with Nick aka Dr. Jasper as she thought over what had transpired with her new boss. She felt calm about what she had done, resign from her position before she even started. She knew Gabe wasn't happy but he would get used to it. After all, he had his chosen reporter there to hold down the fort, she snickered.

She replayed their conversation and felt angry over how he had let Sharleen go like that. He hadn't cared about her feelings or how she was treated by Lucas. The same thing would have eventually happened to her. She didn't want to see Lucas anymore. She didn't feel anything for him like he felt for her. There was no magic. She had thought differently when she first met him. He appeared so warm and friendly with an engaging personality, brilliant smile and handsome features. She was wrong. You definitely can't judge a person by his looks.

She brushed her long dark brown hair and applied her makeup. She put on her favorite silver loop earrings and matching bracelet and necklace. They looked great against her royal blue dress. She smiled and felt warm all over just thinking of Nick. He was the genuine article – warm, engaging, handsome with a beautiful smile, and kind eyes. She didn't remember Lucas' eyes being kind in any way. They were cold like steel. That said something for his inner self.

Gramma Grace peeked into Athena's room and said, "Wow, you look beautiful, sweetheart! You're going to knock Nick's socks off for sure!"

"Oh Gramma Grace! You're too funny!"

"It's an old expression from an old lady. But I know he will be blown away by your beauty, Athena. Are you about ready?"

"Yes, I'll be right out in just a minute."

When she went back to the living room her mother and grandmother were deep in conversation.

"Hey, what's up with you two?"

"Oh, nothing really. We were just discussing how you handled your new boss or ex-boss."

"Do you think I was too forceful?"

"Not at all, dear. You were perfect!" her mother answered with a smile.

"That's right. That man needed to be put into place. He had a nerve to say that he wouldn't fire Lucas even after repeatedly bothering that woman."

"That's what I thought, Gramma. Thank you. I didn't feel comfortable knowing that if that happened to me that is how Gabe would have handled the situation."

"Well, now you will not have to worry about it anymore, honey," her mother said as she gave Athena a hug.

"I do feel better doing that, Mom. Thanks for your support and yours too, Gramma," Athena stated and sighed.

"What's wrong, honey?" Gramma asked with a frown.

"Oh, I was just thinking. Now I have to find another job."

"Yes, but this time you will get an even better one."

"Maybe. Who knows? Something could come along…"

Before Athena could continue with that thought, the doorbell rang.

Carla pushed Athena forward. "Go answer it, dear. It's your young man."

"Oh Mom. Really? He isn't my young man. He is my date."

"But he will be soon." Carla and Grace giggled and watched her open the door. They both gasped when they saw Nick.

"Wow! He's handsome like a movie star," Gramma Grace whispered to Carla.

"Yes, he certainly is!" Carla agreed as she smiled at the way this handsome young man greeted her daughter with a kiss on the cheek.

Athena turned toward her mother and grandmother and pulled Nick along to meet them.

"Mom, Gramma, this is Dr. Nick Jasper."

Carla stepped forward and took Nick's outstretched hand. "Hello, Nick. Nice to meet you."

"It's my pleasure, Mrs. Stone."

"Oh, please call me Carla."

"Okay, Carla."

"And, this is my grandmother Grace."

"Nice to meet you, Grandmother Grace."

"Oh, it's my sincere pleasure, Nick, to meet someone like you, so handsome and such a gentleman."

Nick blushed and shook Grace's hand saying, "Thank you. That's kind of you."

"Oh, I'm not just being kind, Nick. You are movie star handsome."

"Gramma, please."

"What, honey? He is, isn't he?"

"Umm, I think we should go now, Nick."

Nick smiled, nodded and waved to Carla and Gramma as they headed out to dinner.

When they were situated in Nick's car, Athena announced, "Sorry about that. I didn't know they were going to gush all over you."

"No problem. I kind of liked the attention. I don't have a mother or grandmother to fawn over me. It was nice."

"I'm sorry. You don't have a mother or grandmother?"

"No, they both passed – my mother a few years ago and my grandmother several years before. I am a little older than you, Athena."

"Not by much, Nick. I'm 25. You can't be more than 30."

"Thirty-two to be exact, Athena."

"Oh, that's not much at all."

"So, you don't think of me as an old man?"

"No, silly. You are a young man to me and to my family. See how they fell all over you?"

"Yes, it was nice. You're lucky to have them both. I can see where you get your beauty. They are both lovely."

"Thank you, Nick. They would be thrilled to hear that you think they are lovely!" Athena chuckled.

"Not to change the subject but, I made reservations for us at the Italian restaurant, Napolitano's."

"Oh wonderful! I love that place! The chicken parm is delicious!"

"Oh, you've been there already? We can try something else if you prefer."

"Oh no! My mouth is salivating now. You can't do that to me! I have to have my chicken cutlet parmesan!"

"Okay, your wish is my command, my lady." After a short time, Nick happily announced, "Well, here we are!" He looked up in his rearview mirror and frowned.

Athena noticed the frown but didn't ask about it. She responded, "Oh thank goodness. I thought I was going to have to drool all night thinking about my meal."

Nick escorted Athena into the lovely ambiance of Napolitano's. The colors of the Italian flag were everywhere and gorgeous scenes of Italy were displayed over each booth – Capri, Napoli, Positano, Venice and more.

Athena felt like she was in Italy as she admired the paintings and salivated over the delicious smells that filled the air.

Once seated they chose an Italian wine and sat back to enjoy it. They clinked glasses and made a toast. "Here's to us. May we become closer first as friends then maybe more?"

"Friends?" Athena asked.

"Well, I don't want to push myself upon you. I want to get to know you better as a person and become friends, then work from there. I believe you have to like a person before you can learn to love them."

"Yes, I agree, Nick. I like that philosophy."

Nick refilled their glasses as the waiter came to take their orders.

They ordered the same thing, chicken cutlets with penne and a side salad.

"Nick?"

"Yes, Athena. What is it? You looked worried about something."

"No, I'm not. But I noticed that you did look concerned at something you saw in your rearview mirror."

"Oh, it was nothing. I thought I recognized someone behind me."

"Who?"

"Oh, no one you would know. It's okay. No worries, Athena. Here comes our dinner."

They ate in silence enjoying every delicious mouthful. When they were finished drinking more wine, Athena asked Nick, "Who was it you saw?"

"I don't want to worry you. It's okay. I saw this red Mustang behind us all the way from the beach. It followed closely and slowed down when I did. That was a little strange. It disappeared when I turned into the parking lot of the restaurant."

"A red Mustang?"

"Yes. Do you know someone with a red Mustang?"

"Um, yes I do. It's someone I met at the place where I was going to work."

Athena explained what happened about Lucas and her boss and how she resigned before starting her new job.

"Do you think you are in danger from him?"

"I don't know. But it is strange that he was following us. I had lunch with him earlier today and he had asked me to dinner but I refused, of course."

"Well, I'm glad you did. I would have been disappointed if you cancelled our date."

"Oh no, I would never do that. I don't even like him. I was only being polite because I was going to be working with him. Now I won't have to do either."

As Athena finished saying this, Lucas appeared at the door. He looked right at her and headed that way.

"Oh no, speaking of the devil. Here he is!"

"What?" Nick turned to look and saw a disgruntled looking young man heading their way.

A waiter intercepted him and tried to guide him to a table but Lucas pushed him aside and proceeded toward Athena and Nick.

"Well, look who it is – Athena and her date. So, this is the guy you stood me up for?"

"Lucas, what are you doing here? You were not stood up. I had a date already with this gentleman."

"Aren't you going to introduce me?" Lucas stuck out his hand into Nick's face.

"No, I am not, Lucas. Please leave."

"Why should I? I came here to have dinner. It's a free country, Athena."

"Well, then go have dinner and leave me alone."

A waiter came forward when he heard raised voices. "Let me seat you, sir. This way, please."

Lucas grunted and followed the waiter to another table where he sat so he could keep an eye on Athena and her date.

"We should leave, Nick. He is going to make us uncomfortable all evening. We can take our dessert back to my house. Let's go."

"Okay, whatever you want to do, Athena. Let me pay the check and we will leave right away."

"Thank you."

Nick took the dessert from the waiter and helped Athena on with her wrap. He gave her his arm to escort her back to his car.

Once they were on their way Athena said, "Nick take me home to my house, not the beach. He may go back to the beach looking for me. I would feel better at home. I'll call my mother to let her know he may show up there."

"Good idea. I won't leave you alone tonight. He may figure out where you are."

"It's okay. I have an alarm system which I put in after my father…"

"Oh, yes. That was smart, Athena."

They arrived at Athena's apartment and she prepared coffee and laid out the cannoli on two plates.

"Please sit down, Nick. Enjoy your coffee and cannoli. They are exceptional!"

"Mmm, yes they are. Almost as much as you are, Athena."

Their eyes met across the table and their hands reached and touched.

Athena felt a warm tingling sensation travel up her arm, settle in her chest, and radiate down to her limbs, which felt like jelly.

She stood up and pulled Nick along to her bedroom. Their eyes never left each other as they sat on the edge of her queen size bed.

They slipped out of their shoes and stood in front of each other until Athena reached over and began to unbutton Nick's shirt and he in turn worked on the zipper to her dress.

Her fingers fumbled as she pulled off his tie, shirt and ran her hands over his broad and sculptured chest. Nick growled deep in his throat with pleasure at her touch.

He hurried along and pulled her dress up over her head and undid her bra with tenderness. He gazed at her full breasts and sighed. "You are lovelier than I could have ever imagined, Athena."

"You are quite a specimen yourself, Nick. I didn't know you were so muscular and fit."

Nick chuckled, "I guess I'm not so bad for an old man."

Athena laid back and smiled beckoning her little finger at him to join her on her pillow.

"Are you sure you want this, Athena?"

"Yes. I've never been more sure, Nick. I like you and feel a strong connection with you. I want to get closer right now."

"Okay, I aim to please, my lady. As long as you are sure. I don't want to take advantage of you after the wine, and cannoli."

"I didn't have enough of either to feel unsure of anything. So please kiss me!"

Nick came down toward her and kissed her lips softly then more firmly. He caressed her breasts with both hands as they kissed. Athena leaned into his hands and sighed, making strange sounds in the back of her throat.

"Oh, Nick. Please take off your pants."

Nick sat up and pulled off his belt with urgency as Athena helped him take his pants down.

They were unaware of anything else but each other. They did not see the person lurking outside the bedroom window trying to peek in.

CHAPTER TWENTY-NINE

Athena lay content in Nick's arms and dozed intermittently as did he. They both jumped up when they heard a noise outside the window.

"What was that?" Athena asked anxiously.

"I don't know. Let me get dressed and I will check it out."

"Please Nick, don't go outside. It could be him."

"Do you have the alarm on?"

"Yes. You can't open the door or it will go off."

"Okay. I'll just look out the windows and see if his car is there."

"Oh, he wouldn't park it close to the house. He would have parked it further away and walked over. He wouldn't want us to see it. You can't hide a red car like that."

"Yes, you're right about that."

Nick peeked through the curtains in each room but couldn't see anything. There was also no sign of Lucas's Mustang

"Wait a minute, Nick. I forgot to call my mother. Let me call her now and see if he went there first."

"Okay. Relax, Athena. You are safe. I'm not going anywhere."

"Thank you." Athena leaned in and kissed his lips softly.

"Mom? Are you and Gramma okay?"

"Yes, dear. What's wrong? Where are you?"

"I'm at my apartment with Nick. We had to leave the restaurant early because Lucas showed up. Did he go there?"

"No. We didn't see him. Are you all right? Do you want me to call the police?"

"No. I think he's gone now. He was roaming around outside. We can't see him or his car."

"Well, please call me when you plan on coming back here. If you need to call the police, don't hesitate. Okay, honey?"

"I won't, Mom. I promise to call you when I leave here."

"Okay, Athena. Please be careful."

"I will, Mom. Don't worry. Nick is here with me."

"Oh, that's good. He is such a nice man."

"Yes, he is," Athena smiled and winked at Nick.

He leaned close, nuzzled her neck and planted a kiss on her cheek.

"Everything okay there?" Nick queried.

"Yes. They're fine. They never saw him. That doesn't mean he wasn't there. I wouldn't put it past him to sneak around and look in the windows for me. He probably didn't see your car and came here."

"Right, that's probably what he did."

There was suddenly a loud banging on the front door.

Athena jumped back in alarm and looked at Nick. "That's him! He's here. We better call the police. He won't go away."

Nick took Athena into his arms and held her tight. He could feel her trembling.

When the banging became more persistent, "Athena, most definitely we should call the police."

"Wait, maybe I should talk to him and convince him to go away and leave me alone." Athena hastily dressed as Nick did the same.

"I don't think that's a good idea, Athena. He doesn't appear to be a man of reason."

"I know. He is unreasonable, especially knowing how he treated Sharleen."

The banging became incessant, and now Lucas began calling out, "Athena? I know you're in there!"

Athena went out to the hall, leaned against the door and yelled back, "Go away, Lucas or I will call the police."

"We need to talk, Athena. I want to talk to you. Open the door!"

"No, go away, Lucas. I'm warning you!"

"Do you have your boyfriend there? Are you sleeping with him? You're cheating on me?!"

"Lucas, listen to yourself. You are being ridiculous. You and I are not a couple. You have to leave now."

The banging became louder and stronger and the door rattled from the vibrations to make the door separate enough to cause the alarm to go off. It was loud and abrasive causing all to cover their ears and back away from the door.

Athena let it blare out refusing to turn it off until Lucas left. "Leave now or I call the police!"

"Turn it off, Athena. I need to talk to you! Turn it off or I will break in the door!"

"No you won't, Lucas. I'm calling the police."

Athena called the police and reported what was going on over the blaring sound of the alarm. They promised to be there shortly.

Her cell rang right after she put it down. It was her grandmother.

"Athena, honey. Are you okay? I got bad vibes about Lucas. Is he there?"

"Yes, he is. I called the police and they are on their way over now."

"What is that noise?"

"My alarm went off when he nearly knocked down my door."

"Don't let him in whatever you do, Athena. He is dangerous. Is Nick there with you?"

"Yes, he is. But you probably already know that, Gramma Grace, since you are clairvoyant," Athena chuckled.

"Well, yes. I do know that but just making sure," she laughed too.

"We're fine, Gramma. You don't need to worry."

"Okay. Call me after the police leave and take him away."

"I will. I plan on coming up to the beach. Nick will be staying there too."

"That's sound perfect to me, honey."

"Oh Gramma, stop it."

"Hmm, you are a couple now?"

"Yes, Gramma, we are."

"Good to know! Stay safe. I will keep an eye on Lucas for you. He shouldn't be too much more trouble for you. I will take care of him."

"Oh, Gramma Grace. Don't do anything, please. You be careful too."

"Don't worry about me. I can handle myself."

"I know you can. But humor me just the same. Okay?"

"Sure, sweetheart. We will be up when you get here. Call before you leave though. Okay?"

"Will do. I'm having a hard time hearing. This alarm is driving me crazy. I'm going to shut it off.

The company may be trying to get me on the other line. I got to go."

"Okay. See you later."

Athena clicked to end the call and heard a voice, "Hello. Yes, this is Athena Stone. Let me turn off the alarm. I can't hear you."

"Please do. I need your code, Athena."

"Yes. It's 'Second Act.'"

"Good. Is everything all right?"

"Yes, someone was at my door and nearly kicked it in. I called the police already. You don't have to."

"Okay. We did call them already since we couldn't get through to you. Your line was busy."

"Oh, yes. I was on the phone with my grandmother. Sorry. With the alarm on I didn't hear the beep."

"All right. As long as everything is okay. Goodbye. Have a good night."

"Thank you. You too."

"Alarm company?"

"Yes. They're very good. I couldn't hear the beep on my phone when I was talking to Gramma

Grace. When I didn't answer they called the police."

"Okay, so the police will definitely be here shortly."

"Yes, I hope so. Do you see him out there, Nick?"

"I don't see him now but the police just pulled up."

There was a knocking on the door but this time not as loud. Athena looked out and saw two officers standing there looking around.

She opened the door and greeted them in relief. "Thank you so much for coming." She explained what had transpired and they asked if she was okay. When assured that she was safe, they said they would be looking around the yard to see if the man in question was still there.

Athena mentioned his red Mustang, "He may have parked down the street so I wouldn't see his car."

"Okay, we'll drive around after we leave here to see if we spot it."

"Thank you, officers. I appreciate that."

"Good day, Miss and Sir."

Nick stood protectively beside Athena as she had spoken to the police. He nodded to them when they met his eye.

The police circled the house but did not find Lucas. They drove around the block with no sign of a red Mustang. There was nothing else they could do but head back to the precinct.

***

Lucas watched from a neighbor's yard as the police drove away. He had hidden his car in someone's carport down the street hoping that it would not be noticed. He wasn't finished with Athena yet. How dare she spend time with this man! She was probably sleeping with him. He was determined to come between them. After all, Athena was his.

Athena and Nick were unaware that Lucas was still lurking close by. Athena packed up the rest of the cannoli to bring back to the beach for her mother and grandmother and grabbed a couple more bottles of wine. She felt like she would need them to get over this fright from Lucas. There were only a couple left on the rack. She would definitely have to go shopping soon for more.

CHAPTER THIRTY

Athena called her mother to let her know they were on their way back to the beach so they wouldn't worry. Once they arrived, her mother and grandmother were at the door to welcome them in as Athena looked around the street for any sign of Lucas and his car.

They arrived back at the beach and Carla came forward to welcome them back.

"Please come in. Are you both all right? That was quite a fright for you, honey."

"Yes, Mom. I felt Arnold's presence again. It was almost like he was there telling Lucas to frighten me. I know that doesn't sound possible but I don't put anything past him."

"Oh, Athena. That is not too farfetched. But I don't think you have to worry about your father, err, I mean Arnold ever again. The one to worry about now is Lucas. He's definitely unstable if he thinks that he can control you." Gramma Grace stated, with a worried expression. "Someone needs to put him in his place."

"Oh no, Gramma Grace. Please don't do anything. He will get tired of hanging around and eventually give up on me. I'm sorry I even gave him the idea that we were a couple. I'll see you soon."

"Did you give him that idea?" Nick asked with a frown after Athena finished talking to her grandmother.

"No, I don't think I did. I liked him when I first met him and we had a coffee the day that I had my interview with Gabe Forester. Then he came over and took me to lunch yesterday. He was a gentleman and pleasant all during our lunch. He never showed this side of himself to me."

"So you say you liked him then."

"Well, he was nice to me. He was the first person I met at the newspaper. He made me feel welcome. But when Gabe came and told us about his behavior toward a fellow employee it made me wary of him."

"Yes, most definitely you should feel cautious about him," Nick responded.

Carla asked, "How about some coffee to go with whatever you are holding in that box, Athena?"

"Oh, sorry. Yes, I almost forgot. We brought some cannoli from Napolitano's to share with you both."

"Cannoli? I love Napolitano's cannoli! Thank you so much. Let me make some coffee right away," Carla said as she rushed off to brew a pot with the box of cannoli in one hand and the wine in the other.

Gramma Grace whispered to Athena, "Don't worry, sweetheart. I will take care of Lucas. I've always promised to take care of you even after I leave this world."

"Oh Gramma. Don't say things like that. You frighten me. I'm fine. Lucas won't bother me anymore. He will give up."

"Maybe, maybe not. Never mind him. Let's have some coffee and cannoli." Threading her arms through Athena's and Nick's, she guided them to the table where Carla had set with cups, plates and the plate of cannoli.

Nick looked over at Athena and patted her hand. "Everything is going to be all right, Athena. Believe me. If I have to have a serious discussion with Lucas, I will."

"No, Nick. I don't want you to go anywhere near him. He's dangerous." Athena's eyes filled with tears as she pressed Nick's hand.

"Okay. I promise not to seek him out to talk to him. But if he comes back to bother you again, I will."

Athena shook her head and wiped her eyes pleading with him.

Nick put his arm around her trembling shoulders and kissed her cheek. "It's okay. I promise not to do anything."

Athena nodded, smiled wanly and sighed deeply as she sipped her coffee.

Carla changed the subject. "Well, I think this cannoli is still the best I have ever had! Don't you agree, Mother?"

"Yes, I do, dear. It is delicious. Thank you so much for bringing some for us, Nick."

"Oh, no problem. We had them put in a few extras since we were taking them with us to have later. We were quite full after dinner. Right, Athena?"

"Huh? Oh yes, we were full. It was a delicious meal. Thank you so much, Nick. It was lovely."

Gramma Grace could see that Athena was still shaken up and upset over Lucas' actions. She announced, "Listen, I'll make up the bed in the other room for Nick. Ash won't mind you using his room."

"Right. Thank you, Mother. I forgot to do that. You two should get settled in your rooms if you are tired. I'll clean up here."

"Okay, thanks Mom. I could lie down for a little bit. I don't know if I will be able to sleep though."

"Let me help you, Carla. I'm not ready to sleep yet either. I don't want to rush in there until Grace has had a chance to make up the bed."

"Okay. That would be nice, Nick. We could have a little talk and get to know each other especially since you will be around more from now on."

"Yeah. I guess you will be seeing me more. I want to tell you how much I care for your daughter. She is lovely in every way, a kind, caring and warm person."

"Oh thank you, Nick. I think so too. She really cares about you too. I can see it by the way she looks at you. She has had a difficult time lately as you know. Well, you were her psychiatrist and should know all about her father and me and the abuse."

"Of course, but you don't have to talk about it. I am not here as a psychiatrist. I am here as Athena's...I don't know what to call myself - boyfriend?"

"Yes, but maybe more than that. Yes, definitely more than that, Nick." Carla patted his hand and smiled.

Gramma Grace came out of the bedroom and cleared her voice, "Nick, your room is all set if you want to use it."

"Okay. Thank you, Grace. I appreciate you letting me stay here. I don't want to leave any of you alone in case…"

"Yes, we understand and welcome you. It'll be nice to get to know you a little better if you can stay for a while."

"Well, I don't have anything planned tomorrow so I can stay around and take you all out for lunch and/or dinner."

"Hmm, sounds good to me. I am always ready to eat, how about you, Carla?"

"Yes, I take after my mother unfortunately," Carla giggled.

"Good, so it's settled. We will do both lunch and dinner tomorrow. I would like to take Athena for a long walk on the beach in the morning to let her unwind and calm down. Do you think that's a good idea?"

"Most definitely! You are a clever man, Nick. I think our Athena is a lucky girl to have met you," Gramma Grace stated with a wink.

"Well, thank you for the coffee and the room. Good night."

"You're most welcome, Nick. Good night. Sleep well," Carla said.

Grace helped Carla put away the dishes as they discussed Nick and Athena. "He's a wonderful young man for our girl, don't you think so, Carla?"

"Yes, he certainly is. But our Athena needs and deserves someone like him," Carla said as she watched her mother's facial expression.

"Of course she does. He is perfect in my eyes, too."

"What are you conjuring up, Mother? I don't like the look on your face. I've seen that look many times before and it always leads to trouble."

"Don't worry yourself, Carla. I'm just thinking over what I can do to make sure things work out for them."

***

Lucas was on his way back to the beach. He had seen Athena and the man leave and stayed far enough behind them so that they would not see him.

He parked around the corner from the beach house and walked up through neighboring yards to the back of the property. He observed them all in the kitchen and watched as Athena left the room first followed by Grace then the man. He was still upset over not being introduced by Athena to this man. But he would find out who he was on his own.

He had gotten a strange feeling in his body as he had approached Athena's house. He didn't know why he reacted the way he did by banging the door so forcefully. It was almost like someone was doing it through him. He didn't think he was that strong on his own. He had shaken if off until he began to yell. He didn't feel as if he was doing the yelling either. What was happening to him?

***

Grace watched from her bedroom window as the man skulked around the yard peeking in at them. She had to do something. She felt a cold presence as the man came closer to her window. He spotted her and backed away.

She used her powers to push him to leave and watched as he ran away from the house. A short time later he drove by the house in his red

Mustang. She followed him in her mind as he became agitated and pressed the gas pedal down further as his speed increased. A sharp turn was coming up. If he didn't slow down, he would not be able to navigate it safely.

She smiled, watched and waited.

CHAPTER THIRTY-ONE

Carla's phone rang. She turned over in bed to find it, and knocked it off the nightstand.

"Hello. Oh, Ash. Yes, I was sleeping but it's time I get up. What time is it?"

"About 7:30 a.m. I didn't hear back from you last night. I left a message on your phone when you didn't answer."

"Oh, sorry, dear. A lot has happened since I spoke with you the other day." She explained all the details about Lucas and how upset Athena was. She included that Nick was staying there to keep them safe.

"Why didn't you call me right away? I would have come right up to do the same. Is Athena okay now?"

"Yes, she is doing better with Nick here. Well, one man was enough to keep us safe. After all, you had patients and hospitals calls to make. I didn't expect you to come over until this morning anyway."

"Okay, I admit it. I was busy but now I am coming right up."

"Good. I've missed you. See you soon, Ash."

"Love you, Carla."

"Love you too."

Carla got up, dressed and went out to the kitchen to prepare breakfast. Athena and Nick were already there having a cup of coffee and snuggling on the couch.

"Oh, I didn't see you there. Did the phone wake you up too?"

"No, Mom. We have been up for a little while and just talking and sipping our coffees."

"That's good. It was your father. He called to see how we were doing. I told him all about Lucas. I should have told him earlier. He was a little upset with me for not. He's on his way up here now."

"Oh, that's good. It'll be nice to see him. I'll help with breakfast, Mom."

"I'll set the table for you lovely ladies and then get showered and dressed before Ash gets here. I don't want to leave his room in a mess with my clothes."

Gramma Grace came out to the kitchen, passing Nick with a greeting, "Good morning, Nick."

"Good morning, Grace. I'm going to clean up Ash's room. He's on his way up here now."

"Okay. He won't mind you using it, you know. Don't worry about that."

"Well, I'll feel better leaving it neat."

"Good morning, Athena and Carla. I'll give you a hand with the bacon. Nick told me Ash is coming."

"Yes, he called a little while ago. Did you hear the phone?"

"Yes, that's what woke me up. But it was time to get up anyway."

"That's what I told Ash. He was upset over hearing about Lucas."

"You told him, Carla?"

"Yes, Mother. He is Athena's father. I thought he should know."

"No more worries about Lucas. Okay? Let's not talk about him. It's a beautiful day. Let's enjoy it and being together," Gramma Grace stated in a calm voice that was unnerving.

"What have you done, Mother?"

"What? What has she done, Mom?"

"You know your grandmother. She is up to something."

Grace turned on the television ignoring both of them as she watched a scene playing out there.

"What did they say, Gramma? I thought I heard something about an accident in town here."

"Yes, there was an accident not far from here."

Athena came closer to the TV. She gasped as she saw something on the screen. "Oh my God, look! It's Lucas's car! He was in an accident!"

Carla shut off the eggs and bacon and came into the living room to listen to the news about the accident. They watched as a stretcher was being loaded with a body and taken away in a waiting ambulance.

"When did this happen?" Athena asked in a shaky voice.

"Looks like it may have happened sometime last night," Grace announced not meeting her granddaughter's eyes.

"Mom, did you have something to do with this?"

"No, of course not, Carla. Why would I do that?"

"You know why, Mother. Wait a minute. Were you the cause of Arnold's crash too? Oh my God!"

"Don't jump to conclusions, Carla. They both died at their own hands. I had nothing to do with either one. You think I have that much power?" Grace chuckled.

"I don't know what you are capable of, Mother. All I know is that you were scheming to do something and then something happened."

"Just wishful thinking, I guess. I really did not have anything to do with it. Though I did frighten him away when he was skulking around last night at my window."

"What? You saw him in the yard at your window? When was this?" Athena asked in a high pitched voice.

"After everyone was in bed. I looked out my window and there he was walking around close to the house and peeking in each window. I guess when he saw me he got frightened away. I saw him drive away in a hurry past the house."

"What did you do?"

"I told you, Carla. I didn't do anything. He must have gotten spooked by seeing me looking back at him."

"Oh my God. Is he dead?" Athena queried as she got closer to the TV to hear.

"I don't know. It didn't say his condition."

The doorbell rang and Carla went to answer it.

"Ash, thank God you're here. We just heard about an accident. Lucas was in an accident after he left here."

"What? Was he injured? Wait a minute, you said after he left here. He was here?"

"No, I don't know if he was injured. And, yes he was here. Mother said she saw him looking in the window. She frightened him away when he saw her looking back at him."

"Let me call the hospital and find out. Where's Nick?"

"He went to take a shower and clean your room."

Nick heard the raised voices and came out to investigate. "What's going on? I heard Ash's voice and also Athena's."

Athena ran into Nick's arms and held on tight. "He was here, Nick. Lucas was here last night. Gramma Grace saw him and frightened him away. Then he was in an accident."

"What? He was here? An accident?"

"Yes. Dad is calling the hospital to find out if Lucas is all right."

Ash turned to look at the group and shook his head. "He didn't make it. Evidently he was traveling at such a high speed that his car flew off the road and was totaled. He was crushed."

"Oh my God!" Athena collapsed in Nick' arms.

"Athena! Are you all right?" Her father rushed over to see her.

"I'm all right. It was just a shock. The same way that Arnold died in a car crash like I saw in my dream. It happened again! I can't believe it happened again!"

"Sit down, Athena. Please sit down. You are as white as a sheet, sweetheart," her father said as he held her hands, that were ice cold, in his to warm them.

"Mother, explain this please," Carla demanded.

"What is there to explain? He had a terrible accident. He got what he deserved just like Arnold. That's all."

"No, that is not all. You had something to do with each of these accidents, didn't you?"

"No, I did not. They were both unstable individuals who liked to drive fast."

"Mom, please don't yell at Gramma. She had nothing to do with these accidents. How could she?"

Athena met her grandmother's eyes and waited. "Did you, Gramma?"

"No, of course not, honey. I wouldn't be able to do something like that. I am a clairvoyant not a witch."

"Listen everyone. It was a terrible accident. There is nothing any of us can do for Lucas. We can't be blaming anyone for what he did himself. He drove too fast on a sharp turn and it all happened in a second," Ash stated calmly.

"You're right, Ash. I'm sorry, Mother. I didn't mean to accuse you. It was a shock though to have happened just like Arnold's accident. Strange, very strange indeed."

"Well, I think we should finish cooking breakfast and all sit down. We need to calm down," Carla said as she pulled her mother into the kitchen with her to cook.

Athena followed them out to the kitchen and started making toast. "I need a strong cup of coffee. I'll brew another pot. This one is almost empty. Nick and I had a cup or two already."

Everyone settled down to a hearty breakfast but with little discussion about the accident. Instead, they spoke of upcoming nuptials and where they were all going to lunch and dinner later on.

Athena excused herself after clearing the table and went to change for a walk on the beach with Nick.

Gramma Grace followed Athena and stopped at her bedroom door. "Are you all right, honey? You know I had nothing to do with this, don't you?"

"Yes, I believe you, Gramma. But it is quite strange to happen again."

"I guess it was. But now you are free from Lucas and your father. All good things come to those who deserve it."

"That's weird to say, Gramma Grace."

"What? Oh no, it's not really. You have deserved so much better. First your father, then Lucas – you didn't deserve either one. Now you have Nick. Finally you will be happy and your mother too."

"Well, I guess I am fortunate that Nick came along when I needed someone. He is a wonderful man. I really like him."

"Like? Do you mean love?"

"It's too soon to say that word. I think I will one day but not yet."

"You will know when you are ready to say it, Athena. You will know," Gramma Grace smiled and winked at her and went to her own room.

A short time later she and Nick were taking a long leisurely walk on the beach arm in arm. It felt so good to be close to him, Athena thought. She didn't remember ever being so happy with someone.

"Are you feeling better now, Athena?"

"Yes, much better now that I am in your arms, Nick. That's where I always want to be."

"Really? That means you love me?"

"Love you? I…"

"That's okay. You don't have to say it until you are ready. I love you, Athena. I have loved you since the first time I met you. How could I not fall in love with the most beautiful woman in the world?"

"Oh Nick. That is too funny! The first moment…?"

"Well, maybe the second or third but definitely not the fourth," he chuckled and squeezed her tighter.

"Okay, that's more like it. I fell for you…"

"Yes?"

"Well, just now I realized that I do love you, Nick. I love you!"

"Ahh, nicest words I ever heard! I love you too, Athena." Nick turned her toward him and kissed her like she had never been kissed before. She didn't want the kiss to end. She held on tight and kissed him back again and again.

Back at the house Gramma Grace was smiling and hummed as she made up the beds with clean sheets.

***

In between things Athena managed to fit in her appointment with the new psychiatrist, Dr. Carrie Harris.

Dr. Harris was a petite, attractive woman in her mid-thirties with short blonde hair that was in a pageboy cut. She smiled easily with her eyes as she told Athena to take a seat on the couch across from her.

"It's nice to meet you, Dr. Harris." Athena was nervous and her voice raised an octave.

"No need to be nervous, Athena. It's a pleasure to meet you too. Dr. Jasper told me about you and wanted me to continue with your treatment."

They spoke for almost an hour before Athena decided to ask, "Can you put me under hypnosis so I can find out where I was going on the night that I was in an accident?"

"Yes, of course. I thought you didn't want to do that previously, according to your records. What made you change your mind?"

"Well, I am concerned about where I was going and why I was driving so fast. I can't get that out of my mind."

"Yes, I see. Okay. Press the button on the side of the couch and extend the chair back. I want you to relax and take a deep breath and then let it out slowly. Begin counting to 100 and breathe in between. That's it. Now think back to that day that you were in the accident by yourself. What did you do?"

Athena's mind went back to the day of the accident. She remembered receiving a call from her former boyfriend Brian. She couldn't believe he was still alive. She had worried for years that her father may have killed him.

They spoke for a little while and then he began to explain that he had been paid off by her father to leave her alone. He had moved with his family to Michigan where they used to live. He told her that her father had said he would kill him and his family if he didn't move away. He never wanted Brian to contact Athena again. If he did, he would be dead.

Athena shivered as she remembered this. She also was fearful that her father would somehow find out that Brian did contact her after all these years. She asked Brian why he was calling now, so many years later.

He told her that he was going to get married and would be a father in several months. He also had wanted to explain his concern over leaving her so suddenly. He couldn't stop thinking of it and wanted to put his mind at rest and hers too.

She thanked him and wished him well on his upcoming marriage and being a father. She put down the phone and a few minutes later she received a call from her father. He told her that he knew that Brian had called her and that he was a dead man.

Athena didn't know what to do. She tried to call Brian's phone number back to warn him but couldn't get through. What was she going to do?

She got into her car and raced away to see her father.

***

Dr. Harris woke Athena up and asked, "Are you all right?"

"Yes, I know what happened to Brian and why. My father paid him off and told him never to call me. I was on my way to see my father and beg him not to hurt Brian. I guess I was driving too fast and lost control in the rain."

"I see. You never made it to your father's though."

"No, I didn't. Now that he is gone, I will never know whether Brian is okay."

"You could go online and look him up."

"Yes, I could and I will! Thank you so much, Dr. Harris. Part of this mystery is solved. I feel better but not truly better until I know that Brian is safe and well."

"Of course. Well, keep me posted. I don't need to see you until after your parents' wedding. Congratulations to them both. Take care, Athena."

"Thank you, Dr. Harris."

As soon as Athena arrived back home, she looked for Brian Barker online. There he was - handsome and much older since high school with a lovely blonde, pregnant woman on his arm at their wedding in a newspaper announcement. She sighed deeply and thanked God that he was safe.

She didn't want to share this with her family but now knew what had happened. She was relieved and happy for him.

CHAPTER THIRTY-TWO

Athena had been surprised to receive a large square diamond less than a month after she and Nick had started dating. She loved Nick and looked forward to their life together.

She and her grandmother had been planning her mother's and father's wedding all month when Nick announced that he wanted to get married right away too.

When Carla heard this, she suggested that they have a double ceremony. It would save a lot in time and money too. She checked this out with Ash and he was thrilled to share the day with his newfound daughter and his friend and colleague.

Gramma Grace went into full swing planning double of everything. The couples were going to be married on the beach by the pool and have a quiet reception at Napolitano's in their back room with Italian food which they all loved. The owner, Sal Napolitano, was delighted to set it up for them, especially since he got to spend some more time with Grace. He was smitten from the first moment they met to plan the event. Each time Grace had to go finalize something with him, Carla and Athena would giggle. Grace would just roll her eyes and say, "Really? I am an old woman. What would he want with me?"

Carla and Athena would smile and wink at her and say, "I'm sure he'll think of something!" and walk away chuckling.

The day loomed and the weather was beautiful. Grace looked up and said a quiet prayer of thanks. She looked around to make sure no one was there to see her and then waved her hands around for added assurance that the day wouldn't change.

Grace used her powers but never let on what she was truly capable of doing. She didn't want to frighten anyone because sometimes her powers of thought were at times scary to her. All she had to do was think about something and it would happen. She couldn't share what she had done to Arnold and Lucas with Athena and Carla. They may never forgive her even though each man deserved their end.

She sighed and finished up the decorating outside on the trellis with roses and greens. She had placed urns of more roses at each side of the archway where the two couples were to be married.

Sal Napolitano was gracious in giving her flowers for each table at the restaurant for the couples and supplied all the napkins and hors d'oeuvres free of charge. He was such a nice man. She shook her head to get out of the clouds and remonstrated herself for getting romantic and goofy over him.

Her husband had died over twenty years ago from cancer. She never cared to look at another man since, until now. It was sad that Athena never knew her grandfather. He would have been so proud of her. He had been in and out of the hospital when Athena was young. After he died she had moved to Europe to try to get herself together. Now she was glad to be part of Athena and Carla's lives once again.

Carla came up behind her and said, "Lovely, Mother. It's all so lovely! Thank you."

"Oh, you startled me, Carla. I didn't hear you coming. Do you really like it?"

"Oh, yes. It's beautiful and so is the day. We couldn't have ordered one better if that were possible."

"Yes, I agree, dear. You look beautiful, too, in your dress. I love that color blue on you. Is Athena almost ready? Does she need help?"

"Yes, she is almost ready. I helped her put on her gown and did her hair. She looks gorgeous. Thank you for the lovely gown for her. I am so happy for Athena to have found such a wonderful young man. I really love Nick."

"I do too. They make a lovely couple; both are beautiful inside and out. As for the gown, I saw it one day in the shop downtown and had to buy it once I knew they were going to get married. By the way, Carla, you did a good job with Athena, dear."

"Thank you, Mother. But you did help me, you know, even though it was long distance."

"Well it was all in her head that she had me close. I always told her to just think of me and I would be there for her. I didn't really mean I would be there in body, just in spirit. Athena always had a marvelous imagination."

"Well, whatever you did helped her become secure and confident even though our home was anything but."

"I know, Carla. I did all I could to keep him away from you but he was strong in spirit and fought me."

"What do you mean fought you, Mother?"

"Oh, never mind. It's not important now. He is no longer with us, thank goodness. Now you have a wonderful man too, Carla. You are both blessed."

"Yes, Mother. We are! I'm grateful for Ash. I don't know what I would do without him. He makes me happy and I feel so safe and secure with him for once in my life."

"That's good to hear, Carla. I'm happy for you. You are now financially secure too with the sale of the house and the money Arnold left you."

"Yes. I was also surprised we had that much in the bank. He ever let on that we were that financially secure."

"Well, I better see if Athena needs any more help. You call the docs and see if they are on their way here with the Justice of the Peace."

"Okay, I better. They may lose track of time if I don't."

Before Carla could find her phone and call, Ash, Nick and the Justice of the Peace were at the door.

"Carla, you look beautiful!" Ash gushed as he took her in his arms.

"It's not good luck to see the bride before the ceremony, Ash."

"No problem, we are going right out to the beach and will wait for you to come out. I brought a recording of music to introduce you both," the Justice of the Peace announced.

"Thank you… I don't know your name. Sorry."

"Oh, forgive me. This is Dr. Oden Barclay. He was kind enough to offer to perform the ceremony."

"Oh, thank you, Dr. Barclay."

"Please, call me Oden. I know it's an odd name but that's what I'm stuck with," he smiled and shook Carla's hand.

Nick led Oden out to the beach area that was decorated with a rose covered trellis and archway and a few chairs.

"I'll be outside waiting for you, my love." Ash leaned in and gave Carla a quick kiss so as not to mess her makeup.

Grace stopped at the doorway to Athena's room and gasped. "You look beautiful, Athena! Absolutely beautiful!"

"Oh, thank you, Gramma Grace, and also for this absolutely gorgeous gown! I am a little nervous."

"You are welcome, sweetheart. That is to be expected, Athena, that you would be nervous..

Wait a minute, you need something old and something new, something borrowed and something blue."

"Yes, I am all set with something blue. Mom gave me a blue handkerchief. It's also old and borrowed. That takes care of three things."

"Okay, then you need something new." Grace reached into the pocket of her dress and pulled out a sparkling silver cross with diamonds.

Athena's eyes opened wide. "Gramma Grace, where did you get that?"

"I bought it many years ago and wanted my granddaughter to wear it on her wedding day. It will keep you safe always even after I am gone from this world. All you have to do is hold it in your hand and think of me."

"Oh, Gramma Grace! It would be like when I was just a child and all I had to do was think of you and say your name and you were there."

"Yes, sweetheart, just like that. I will always be near."

"You aren't planning to go anywhere, are you?"

"No, of course not. I am too cantankerous to leave this world yet, and don't plan on going too far away from you and your mother. In fact, I found a nice little cottage here at the beach and put down a deposit."

"You did? When was that?"

"Well, the last time I went over to Napolitano's to finalize things for the dinner, I saw this little place on the way there. It was perfect for me. I called the realtor, looked it over and signed the papers. It's mine!"

"That's wonderful, Gramma. I am so happy for you."

"Well, I had to have a place of my own. I can't live with my daughter and her new husband, can I?"

"Mom wouldn't mind at all. You could even stay with us at Nick's place until we find a permanent place or use my apartment. I haven't cancelled my lease yet."

"No, dear. You are newlyweds or will be soon. Let's go get your mother and see if they are ready for you both."

The doorbell rang as Grace led Athena to the living room to sit with her mother until they heard the music cue to come outside.

Standing at the door were Athena's two best friends, Lacy and Fran with their dates.

Athena jumped up and ran over to greet them. "I didn't know you were coming today."

"Your grandmother called and told us about your wedding. We couldn't miss this for all the world," Lacy announced as she hugged Athena.

"You look beautiful, Athena! Wow! Are we late?" Fran said as she hugged Athena next.

"No, not at all. My mom and I are waiting to be summoned. I'm so happy to see you both. Thank you for coming."

Grace led the two couples out to their seats and introduced them to the soon-to-be grooms and Justice of the Peace. When all were settled, Oden started the music for the brides to come outside.

Mother and daughter escorted each other out and walked arm in arm holding their bouquets with their other hands.

Ash and Nick each took a deep breath and let it out slowly when they saw the visions of beauty that were heading their way.

The ceremony went smoothly and the day was warm and sunny. Grace looked up and smiled and nodded her thanks to Him for making this day so special.

The reception was lively and fun with plenty of champagne and delicious Italian food that kept coming. Sal Napolitano was a perfect host and made sure his servers were there continuously topping off glasses of champagne and bringing more food when needed.

Grace smiled at Sal and even danced with him a few times when he nudged her to do so. She felt relaxed and secure that finally both of her girls were safe and she didn't need to take any further action to protect them. This didn't mean that she would ever let down her guard, for you never know when you will need some help from a witch.

She smiled and sipped her champagne, happy to keep her secret from her girls. She looked over at Athena who was touching her cross that glowed a brilliant white light. It would do that each time that Grace thought of her or sensed that Athena needed her help. She had told Athena that she would always be near if she held the cross in her hand.

Athena looked up and smiled and blew a kiss to her Gramma Grace who in turn blew one back.

Carla smiled too when she saw the interchange. She blew one at both of them. She watched her mother with that odd look she always had when she was up to something. She only hoped that trouble wasn't close by once again. But if it was, she knew her mother would take care of it.

CHAPTER THIRTY-THREE

Athena picked up her phone and looked at the text – it was from Brian. He said, "It's a Boy!" She giggled in relief.

"What's so funny, Athena?" Nick queried as he brought her out onto the dance floor.

"Oh, it's a text from an old friend who just had a baby."

"That's nice. Anyone I know?"

"No. It was a long time ago." She smiled as he took her into his arms.

"Are you happy, Athena?" Nick asked as he spun her around on the dance floor once again.

"Oh, how could I not be? I have the handsomest man here who loves me for who I am. He makes me feel safe and secure. I am happier than I have ever been in my life."

"That's what I want to hear, my love. I want to do everything to make you happy, beginning right now."

Athena stopped dancing and looked at him with an arched brow. "What are you up to, Nick? What did you do?"

"Why does it have to be something negative? I want to give you a wedding gift."

"Oh, I didn't get you anything."

"But you did. I have you. You are the best gift I could ever hope for, Athena."

"What did you get me?"

"Oh, now your curiosity is piqued?"

"Yes, it is."

"Okay, I won't keep you in suspense anymore. Here." Nick handed her an envelope that was sealed.

"What's this?"

"Open it and find out." He smiled and waited.

"Oh my! We are going on a honeymoon to Italy?"

"Yes, but that is not all. Look further inside the envelope."

"Oh, oh, wow! You bought a beach house? It's a very large beach house! When did you do all this?" She said as she looked at the photo of a large colonial house with a long frontage right on the beach and the papers to go with it.

"Well, I've been busy. I signed papers today on the house and finalized the honeymoon plans this morning. I hope you like both."

"Are you kidding? What wouldn't I like? I have never been to Italy and always wanted to go."

"I know. Your grandmother told me that you wanted to go since you were young."

"She did, did she? It always seems that Gramma Grace is in the middle of things."

"She only wants the best for you. She bought a place for herself at the same realtor. I saw it. It's small and cozy and perfect for her."

"Yes, she told me about that before the ceremony. I'm happy for her. I had asked her to come live with us if she didn't have a place yet."

"That's funny. I did the same thing. I really like your grandmother. She is a good woman with a heart of gold like your mother."

"Yes, I am fortunate to have them both. Now we will all be living in the same community and close by. Thank you so much, Nick. I love you."

"I love you too, Athena."

Grace smiled as she looked at the newlyweds. She could tell by the happy expression on Athena's face that Nick had given her his wedding gifts of a honeymoon and a house. He had asked Grace a few days ago what Athena would like.

She turned her attention to Carla and Ash. They were beaming with joy and love. She winked at Ash as he smiled her way. She had told him to book a trip to Italy too. Neither couple would know about the other but would see each other on the plane and stay in the same hotel. She knew that this would make both her girls happy to be close to each other but still have space.

Unbeknownst to them, Grace also booked a limo to take the couples to a swanky hotel tonight and then to the airport in the morning.

Sal came over to Grace and held out his hand to her for a dance. She happily took it and snuggled into his arms. She was going to be busy herself with her new beau while the couples were away. He didn't know it yet but she was smitten with him too.

She would have to be careful to keep her secret from him. It could frighten him away if he knew she was a woman of many powers. She smiled as he twirled her around the dance floor.

The End

ABOUT THE AUTHOR

J. E. Spina is a retired administrative secretary from a public school system in Massachusetts. She has always loved writing poetry, novels and children's stories.

This is the fourth novel that J.E. Spina has published. She also has a short story collection written under J.E. Spina.

She has published 16 children's stories and 12 middle-grade novels under Janice Spina. Janice is working on a YA fantasy series, a historical novel and four books in a new mystery series.

Website: http://Jemsbooks.com
Twitter: http://twitter.com/janice_spina
FB Main Page: http://facebook.com/janice.spina.9
FB Author Page: http://facebook.com/janicespina7
FB Novelist Page: http://facebook.com/jespina7
Blog: http://Jemsbooks.wordpress.com

J.E. Spina lives in New Hampshire with her husband, John, and two tanks of fish. John is the illustrator of her children's books and designer of her book covers.

If you enjoyed this book, please leave a review where you purchased it and spread the word about it. J.E. Spina loves to hear from readers and welcomes reviews from wherever her books are purchased. She says, "It's like Christmas each time I receive a review!"

If you would like to be on J.E. Spina's email list to receive updates, newsletters, and special deals on books, please send a request to jjspina@comcast.net and put in subject line **JEMSBOOKS MAILING LIST**.

A NOTE FROM THE AUTHOR

I began writing this book in 2018. It came to me in a dream as most of my stories do. I put it aside to complete other books and didn't look at it until 2020. I usually begin with a title but this time the title kept changing in my mind. I finally decided on this title and the story and characters took over.

Thank you for purchasing one of Jemsbooks. I appreciate your kind support of me and my books.

If you like this book, a review would be greatly appreciated wherever you purchased it. Reviews and word of mouth are the best way to spread your thoughts about books. Please share your review with friends and family. I would love to hear from you. You can reach me at jjspina@comcast.net.

All my books are available on Amazon and Barnes & Noble.

Watch for more books coming for all ages.

With Blessings & Love,

J.E. Spina